Pick Us, Daddy

Pride Pet Play 2023 Series

TL Travis

Sapphire Publishing

Published by Sapphire Publishing

Formatting by TL Travis

Cover by: Covers by Jo

https://www.facebook.com/groups/571551797007649

Photographer: Golden Czermak

https://furiousfotog.com/

Cover Model: Kevin R. Davis

https://www.instagram.com/kevinrdavis.official/

Trigger warning:

There is a scene where one of the MCs recounts an act of abuse that resulted in sexual assault to the police. It is brief with minimal details, but if that is a trigger for you, please don't read this book. Your mental health is far more important to me.

Dedication:

To all my zany friends out there – let your freak flags fly!
I know I have and I've never been happier
What makes us unique is what sets us apart from the rest.
Stay true to you.
Love,
TL

Pick Us, Daddy is part of the Pride Pet Play 2023 multi-author series. Each book can be read as a standalone, but why not check them all out? If you like playful pets who are sometimes naughty, Pride parades, and Daddies who love their boys unconditionally you'll fall in love with our pack!

Blurb

Being in love with your best friend isn't recommended.

Especially when you both prefer to let someone else take control. We knew we were meant to be together, with another, and both had dreams of the perfect Daddy who'd want us both, though he hadn't come along yet.

Riya Cox and Stefan Pierce's friendship didn't start out the conventional way. Nope. It happened when Stefan stepped in after a wanna be handler attempted to coerce Riya into something he didn't want. When he raised his hand to strike Riya, Stefan jumped in and nearly ripped it off. Needless to say, they were banned from that club.

Jonovan Duarte was tired of boys donning masks they weren't meant to wear, used only to appease wealthy Daddies. Was honesty a virtue no longer possessed? Boys would come and go, each having the same goal—to max out his credit cards. With debt gone, along with the sugar babies Jonovan returned to the scene only to go home empty handed. Was it time to call it quits and accept that fate had no match for him?

Contents

Chapter One

Jonovan

"Well, that was a bust," I sighed heavily and mumbled loud enough my friend Steve could hear me. He'd been trying his best to help me find a new pup since the last one crashed and burned, maxing out my credit cards along the way. Damn, I was a fool for that boy, and he fucking knew it. Six months later, Stellan and his new beau were off on the trip of *our* dreams, and I footed the bill for it. Wasn't until my credit card company alerted me that I neared my limit that I knew something was wrong. I'm disputing the charges, well, on all but the room since it was my dumbass that booked it then selectively forgot to cancel after Stellan moved out. But fucking hell, would the betrayal always hurt this much?

"Come on, Jonovan," Steve said as he nudged my shoulder with his. "Let's hit the diner, my treat."

We'd both been members of the Blue Underground, a local BDSM club, for several years now. While Steve preferred to play with those only desiring an occasional scene as opposed to having their own handler, I on the other hand was a serial monogamist. Nurture and guidance were my game. Building a solid foundation with goals toward a long-lasting relationship.

Forever the fool I was.

"Why does it have to be so hard?" I asked aloud though to no one in particular, but Steve stood beside me and as soon as the words left my mouth, I regretted it. Didn't take long for the twelve-year-old boy in him to surface.

"That's what he said," Steve laughed at his own joke. "I'm a funny fucker."

"Hardy, har, har. What are we, twelve?" I chided, though my words held no weight. Hell, I wanted to laugh at his stupid antics myself yet somehow refrained.

"Maaayyybbbeee," he drew the word out. "Come on, I'm hungry."

"Who's a good boy? Who's a good boy?" we heard one of the handlers say. I loved to come watch during pet playtimes, though I longed for one of my own again. I couldn't decide if doing this sated me, albeit temporarily, or if I was a sadist and enjoyed the painful reminder that I was alone. But this was one of my favorite times and on days like today where work was beyond stressful, watching the pets play tended to brighten it.

Steve smirked as he stood beside me. "That guy is wasting his time."

"What's their story?" I asked because it sounded like Steve knew more.

"No clue. They're new and the puppy won't let anyone near his kitten. If I were that guy I'd back off and quit trying. He's wasting his time," Steve repeated.

I turned and watched the awkward interaction while Steve walked ahead of me toward the front exit. Sure enough, as the guy neared, the puppy lurched and nearly nipped his arm.

"Bad dog," the guy scolded, though the puppy showed no remorse. In fact, the pup's growl grew louder, and I nearly stepped between him and the handler in the pet's defense. If he'd have raised his hand to the pup, I wouldn't have thought twice about knocking him on his ass.

"You'll never get anywhere with them," another handler in the arena said to him. "Those two come together and those two leave together and nobody ever goes with them. I have yet to see that pup let anyone near his kitty." My eyes followed his gesture over to the corner where the kitty in question was half curled up, mid back arched like it wasn't sure if it wanted to fight or flee. My heart went out to the scared feline, whatever happened to him in the past was clearly traumatic.

"Why do they come here then? I don't understand. I heard they were kicked out of several other clubs for this shit," said the idiot scolding the pup for bad behavior versus taking the time to be a true handler and learn more about them before he jumped into the deep end. Handler rule number one, get to know your pets first before you take the reins.

"Who knows," the guy who butted in said with a shrug. "I found a couple over here willing to play. Let's go." As soon as they were a good distance away, the puppy returned to his kitty and nudged him with his nose. The kitty circled a couple of times then curled up in a ball as the puppy protectively lay in front of him. Not having ever witnessed such an act, at least not during playtime, it both intrigued and brought forth my protective Daddy side. The carpet squares beneath them did nothing for their bare knees. My mind whirled with the proper gear they needed, the mental shopping cart filled as I got ahead of myself. I was one who tended to overdo where my boys were concerned and though these two didn't belong to me, the urge to take care of them was heavy.

"Jonovan, I'm starving. Let's go," Steve whined from the doorway, still dressed in the suit he wore to work today. The damn man was nowhere near starving and yet he chose to act like a child.

I glimpsed the puppy in question, he cocked his head to the side and eyed me. Were his floppy ears burning as he gauged my next move? Or was he merely curious about the stranger equally as enthralled with him and his...friend? Partner? They would be an anomaly for sure if they were in a relationship without a Dom/Daddy. Our sharp gazes remained laser focused on one another, daring the other to make the first move. Would he allow me near them? Or only close to him? Would he lash out and try to bite me? No, now was not the time to broach that. It was best to leave things as they were and speak with Artesia, the owner of the Blue Underground, first. She may have insight into their dynamic. Plus, I needed to get to her before those two guys the pup just had the negative interaction with had a chance to complain. There was definitely something more going on and the overwhelming desire to get to the bottom of it grew with each passing moment.

Before Steve had a chance to whine again, I nodded to the pup, letting him know he had been noticed but I was leaving so it was okay to stand down. His kitty was safe.

My thoughts never strayed the entire drive to the restaurant, albeit it wasn't that far. But I'd not witnessed such an act before as I had with those two. Curiosity wasn't really the way to explain the desire, more like I was interested in the role of therapy Daddy. To draw them from their shells and show them that not everybody was the big bad wolf and although I didn't know if that were the case, instinct led me to believe I was right—they had been hurt in the past. At least the kitty had been, or so I assumed and generally when I went with my gut, it was always right. Well, at least about everything but winning lottery tickets, it would appear. I had an uncanny knack for being spot on when it came to things that were negative and just once I'd like to be right about something that was positive. *Hint, hint, lottery gods, how about that winning ticket?*

Steve beat me to the restaurant and checked in to a twenty-five-minute wait. Neither of us paid much attention to the clock or the fact that it was the latter half of the dinner rush time. He typed away on his phone while my thoughts remained focused on the boys.

"What gives?" Steve asked as soon as we'd given the waitress our orders.

"What do you mean what gives? What are you talking about?" I asked, though I already knew where this was headed.

"I saw you watching those two. After the negative interaction with the puppy, I'm sure those guys will complain to Artesia. They'll be booted out after that. I have to say, I haven't seen you this intrigued with a pet for quite some time, and I know you well, my friend," he pointed his fork at me. "What's that devious little mind of yours plotting?'

"Devious? I don't have a devious bone in my body," I scoffed.

“No, but you do get bored easily,” Steve pointed out. I wish he hadn't. “It’s obvious those two require a full-time handler, someone in it for the long haul who will be able to pull the proverbial bone out of that puppy's ass. You work long hours, Jonovan. Do you have the time it will take to devote to them? Plus, what if they’re an established couple? And if so, why would they go to a club to play instead of doing it at home?”

“There's something more going on here, Steve, and I’m interested to find out. And as you pointed out, if those guys complained to Artesia, I won’t get the chance to. I’ll reach out to her and try to stall, buy some time,” I shared my thoughts aloud. “They could be a couple but, ugh, I’m not even sure what.”

“You looking for a challenge or something, big guy?” He laughed. “’Cause you’re about to open Pandora’s box of pet play nightmares and I hope you’re ready for it.”

“You know, I don't want to call it a challenge, though I'm always up for one. These are humans we’re talking about and to label it as such feels cold and uncaring. I won’t deny there is something about them that spoke to me in a way I can't explain. Almost like they needed me on this bone deep level. Who knows,” I said as I tossed my napkin down. “I'm no therapist but I would like to see if I could be what they need.”

“Spoken like the true Daddy you are,” Steve smirked. “Go get your boys.”

They weren't my boys, though I couldn't deny the thrill that shot through me at Steve's words. As I got home, I shot off an e-mail to Artesia that recapped what I'd witnessed and let her know I'd like the opportunity to work with them if they were in fact looking for a handler. I didn't expect a return response at this late hour, but I could not get those two off my mind and I had to at least take a step forward or I'd forever wonder if I missed a golden opportunity. Maybe I wasn't the right Daddy for them, but at the very least I could possibly help them with whatever problem they had so they could find the right handler. Although I didn't know for certain if they were a romantic couple or just friends, for my own sense of peace I needed to find out.

Showered and with the house locked up, I slid into bed and grabbed my iPad, giving my work emails one last check before I called it a night. I wasn't the workaholic I once was but being the owner of a maintenance company made it a hard habit to break. In the beginning I was a solo tech, branching out on my own. Wrench in hand and a smile on my face, I literally went to the neighbors then branched out into the commercial realm, selling my abilities. Many jobs I did for free—word of mouth was everything in this industry—and from that my client base was established. I'd never forget those days, twenty years ago, though it felt like yesterday. My body now had the aches and pains to match the long, hard hours I'd put in.

In the beginning, I worked out of my parents' house while I took night classes at the community college in business management. For as long as I could remember, I would tinker away. My dad taught me everything I knew and although he was retired now, I still ran industry anomalies past him. Dad thrived on challenges and for me to get to the heart of what made something tick held the same value. Even if I thought I knew the answer I still wanted Dad's opinion. Between the two of us we could pretty much figure out how to fix damn near anything. Facilities. Once it's in your veins it stays. Hell, I couldn't go to a restaurant without mentally picking it apart. *When was the last time they had their air filters changed? Is that mold on the restroom ceiling?* And OSHA violations, don't even get me started.

Although in the day-to-day business aspects, I wasn't hands-on anymore—I left that to my team of capable mobile techs—I still had an itch to scratch and would get the old tool belt out. Duarte Maintenance Solutions covered a territory of four states in the southwest and my office staff managed everything else. They didn't need me for the daily operations, but being the control freak that I was it was difficult to relinquish the reins.

I just needed something more in my life, or someone to occupy my time with. Then I could slowly phase out and stop driving my staff insane.

I lived a comfortable life. I bought my house as a fixer upper fifteen years ago. Dad and I along with a couple of my lead techs fixed it up, although it wasn't as fast as it sounds, and it nearly drained my savings. Start to finish, it took over a year to complete but I loved the old house. It had great bones, was ugly as sin when I found her but now, she was the belle of Beacon Street and I loved it. One of the wisest investments I'd made to date was now worth so much more than what I'd originally paid.

I reached over to shut off the light on the nightstand when my e-mail notification pinged. I was surprised to see a return email from Artesia at this late hour.

Jonovan,

As you know, I'm not at liberty to share information on any of our club's members, though I will let you know that those two come with a gentle word of warning. If you sincerely want to meet with them, I can reach out and see if they're interested.

You've taken on some tough boys in the past and things always ended amicably. You've caused no problems and I'm appreciative of that. I too am curious to find the root cause for these boys' reactions. Usually, it's a Dom that gets ejected from a club and rightfully so, but pets? Something doesn't add up here and I hope these boys agree to meet with you. If anyone can get through to them, it's you. We'll talk soon.

Until then,

Artesia

"Well," I said to my beloved boxer, Titus, "that's a start, boy. Now all we can do is wait for them to make the next move." He curled up beside me, his head didn't so much as hit the bed before he was snoring. And dear God, the flatulence. It's a damn good thing I loved that smushy face as much as I did. That boy smelled like he was rotting from the inside out. The urge to hang one of those pine tree fresheners from his nubby tail was strong, though I'm sure once it got bouncing around, he'd launch it across the room. I sighed, resigned to the fact my sinuses would never be the same. "Goodnight, my stinky pup. I love you."

Chapter Two

Stefan

Wanted

A loving Daddy for a pup and his kitty.

Well, mostly.

Occasional diva moments, but nothing too serious.

Loves to cuddle.

Both have a praise kink.

Though the pup is not opposed to dirty talk and spankings.

"What are you doing, Stefan?" Riya asked as he walked up behind me. I was sitting at our rickety two-person dining table we'd saved from a tragic dumpster death. Though lately I'd wondered if it wasn't better off at the dump becoming mold fodder.

"I'm submitting a *Daddy wanted* ad to Artesia for the virtual bulletin board on the Blue Underground's website in the hopes she can help us find a Daddy. A real one who understands how to handle us as opposed to the jerks who just want to jump right in with their own agenda." No further explanation was needed, Riya and I had had our share of those fucknuts and were over it.

"Yeah," he sighed. "I didn't like that guy last night. He was scary," Riya said as he took a seat on my lap, my arms protectively wrapped around my best friend as I hugged him tight.

"I know, sweetheart, and I'm sorry that he scared you. But back to the ad, do you think it says too much about us? I read it like a thousand times before I settled on this version," I said, hoping that assured him I wasn't rushing into anything. Riya and I loved each other and any Daddy who wanted us got the pair—that was non-negotiable.

"I think we're gonna get a lot of dick pics using the profile picture of us wearing nothing but our harnesses and those skimpy shorts. I think the freaks are going to come out of their closet howling and we may get more than we bargained for," Riya said.

"I'm tired of playing at home. When we go to the club all we get are jerks. Why can't we have a loving, sexy Daddy of our own?" It was like the ultimate wish we both shared.

Well, Riya wanted a handler, but I wanted a Daddy handler.

"I don't know if I'm ready, Stefan," Riya whispered.

"And playing at home isn't fun anymore. I'm tired of having our playtime interrupted by Mrs. Fletcher hitting the ceiling below with a broom because we've interrupted her soap operas. Yes, she's got the volume on the TV up so loud you can hear it throughout the entire building yet somehow our bounding around bothers her." I had no words. The woman was deaf as anything yet could hear us even with our knee pads on.

"Yeah, the first time she said it sounded like a rumpus room up here I had to Google what rumpus was," Riya giggled.

"I don't even think that word is in the dictionary anymore," I shrugged. "Well, here goes nothing." I posted it and shut down the laptop. Riya hopped off and went to shower. We both had to work tonight. Our jobs weren't glamorous, but they paid the rent on our studio apartment. Had we not been as close as we were we'd never have been able to live in such close proximity and share a bed. The two of us had grown to rely on one another over the years, neither having had the best experiences before we met.

Six years ago, at the mall food court was where it all started. I was job hunting, filling out applications at every place that would let me. Riya had just started working at the hot dog stand and was miserable. One thing led to another, and we both landed jobs at one of the clothing stores in the same mall. Now, Riya was a shift lead, and I was a team lead in men's clothing. Neither job was full-time because what retailer wanted to give their employees benefits? But you know, we got just enough hours that the corporate office didn't complain, and we paid our bills. While our schedules didn't always align, for the most part we worked the same shifts. Neither of us drove but thankfully the mall was within walking distance.

"Riya, look," I held my phone up so he could see it. "Looks like we're getting kicked out of another club." I scowled at the screen, recognizing Artesia's name.

"Might as well answer it," Riya said. "Sorry."

"Don't you dare apologize. I'll always protect you until the very end." I hated it when he did that, it wasn't his fault by any means, and I swore I'd never let another person hurt him again.

I pressed the answer button and put her on the speaker as we walked home. "Don't worry, we won't say anything. We will go quietly," I said instead of answering like a normal human with a simple hello.

"Well, hello to you, too, sweetheart," Artesia replied.

"Sorry," Riya again said, though this time it was meant for Artesia's ears.

"While I won't pretend like nothing happened, I would like to speak with the two of you if you have a few moments?" Artesia asked. Apprehension was the best way to explain the look Riya and I exchanged.

"Um, okay," I replied.

"I don't follow another's lead, I run my club my way with the health and safety of our members first and foremost. Depending on the incident, I'm not always quick to ban. Certain things are intolerable but protecting another isn't as cut and dry. But I have a proposition for the two of you," she paused.

"We're listening." In my mind I only heard, *here we go again*.

"There's another member of the club, a long time, upstanding man who is a handler. He has asked if he could work with the two of you. Normally, I don't get involved in client meetings but given your history and what happened during your last visit I told him I'd need to speak with you both first. I know you are a pair and not to be separated, he is aware of this also and has no qualms with that. Would the two of you be interested in meeting with him?" she asked.

The terror on Riya's face nearly had me spouting out my normal *no* reply but given this was Artesia, the only club owner around who hadn't kicked us out after something as simple as nearly biting another, gave me pause. This warranted a conversation between Riya and me. "Could you give us a moment, Artesia?"

"Absolutely. If you'd like, you can discuss it and call me back. No rush and if you do decide to meet with him, I'll open the club a couple of hours early for a private meet and greet."

"You'd be willing to do that for us?" I asked, stunned that anyone would be so nice to us. In the past we hadn't been allowed to tell our side, just got kicked out while the assholes remained.

"Absolutely. You boys talk it over and let me know. Enjoy your night," Artesia said and then hung up. Riya and I stared blankly at the phone, as though we'd seen a ghost.

Riya said nothing during the rest of the walk and immediately went into the bathroom to change while I got dinner started. A few minutes later, he appeared wearing his favorite footie pajamas. "Finish stirring the sauce while I get changed." He took over cooking duties while I stripped down to my boxers and a t-shirt.

"Riya," I began as soon as we sat down to eat. "You know I'll never leave you alone with another man. Ever. There won't be another Dominic. I'll protect you with my life. I love you."

Riya sighed and swirled his noodles. "I know. It's just..." he trailed off and I didn't butt in. Riya needed to gather his thoughts and find his strength to get through this. We were lonely. Sure, we had each other but our dynamic in the bedroom wasn't complete, nor was our pet play scene.

We were subs in both aspects and would always feel like something was missing until we found the right Daddy. Was this guy him? Who knew, but we'd never find out if we didn't try. "Do you really think it will be okay? That she honestly wants to help us? Well, help me?"

"You had it right the first time, help us. We are a team and if a Daddy can't or won't take both of us and treat us equally then he's not the daddy for us. End of story. The fact that Artesia reached out and offered to give us an opportunity, something no one has ever done, says a lot about her. We know our limits and they're non-negotiable. We will not be ignored again. We have a voice, and it will be heard. If a Dom steps one toe over that line, we tap out," I assured Riya and I meant every word.

Riya went silent again, slowly slurping down his spaghetti. The wait killed me, I really wanted to do this. This kind of opportunity, for someone in the scene to give us a chance and see that we weren't bad was a one in a million. Yeah, I had been naughty, but it was all with good intentions and if someone would just hear our side of the story that would change. Well, maybe...but we were nothing without hope.

"Just meet, right? We're not diving right in and calling him Daddy or selling our souls to the pet world devil, are we?" Riya asked.

"Just meeting with him, Riya. Nothing more, I promise," I did my best to assure him though on the inside my pup bounced around like mad.

"Okay," he nodded, "call Artesia and set it up. You know my schedule." Riya sighed and stood up. "I'll do the dishes." When Riya offered to do the dishes, it was code for, *I'm so deep in my own head I'm not fun to be around so please, just leave me alone.*

I started a load of laundry and straightened up around the ten-by-ten apartment. Well, it wasn't that small, though it sure did feel like it. Especially at times such as this when we both needed separate rooms to go to. In the space we had a four-drawer dresser, queen-sized bed, small two-person couch, and the dinner table. Just like everything else in our relationship, we made the cramped area work the best we could.

Riya and I showered separately. The tiny shower and tub in the bathroom couldn't hold two bodies in it at the same time. I swore at times we were like an old married couple—work, dinner, shower, bed. We literally had next to no nightlife. Hell, we'd never actually been members at the clubs. With each one we'd barely used our free passes before we were asked to leave. I was surprised as non-members that Artesia was willing to help us at all. We'd paid her nothing, and we honestly couldn't afford the membership and were hoping to only pay the entrance fee to attend pet play nights. Even that would stretch our lack of budget.

Having tomorrow off meant we could sleep in. I grabbed our shared iPad off the dresser and opened the book I was currently in the middle of. Riya curled up against my side and dozed right off. I was envious of his ability to immediately fall into a deep sleep. For me, I needed a way to shut my brain down and generally, reading did that for me.

It wasn't too long after I'd called it a night and fell asleep that I was awoken. Riya thrashed around beside me yelling *No! Stop! Red!* I didn't need to ask to know what brought this on. The deadly thoughts I had of what I'd like to do to Dominic consumed me with such rage that had I acted on the anger I'd be in jail and would secure a prime seat on the bus to hell.

"Sssh, Riya, you're okay," I whispered to him. "You're safe." He cried and kicked, so deep into this nightmare. *No! Stop!* he repeated. Gently, I shook his shoulder, and tried my best to not startle him. "Riya, baby, it's me, Stefan. I'm right here, you're okay." He fisted my shirt and began to sob uncontrollably. I wrapped my arms around him and repeated, "You're okay, baby. I'm right here, you're okay. The bad man's gone," until he calmed down. I kissed the top of his head while I rocked him until he fell back to sleep. "I love you, Riya. Nobody will ever hurt you again."

Riya woke the next morning before me and while I felt the bed shift, I was too exhausted to move. I slept a bit longer and woke later to the smell of bacon, which I truly believe that amazing scent would wake anyone. Well, that and coffee, which I think I smelled, too.

"Morning," I'm said through a yawn as I wiped my eyes.

"Good morning," Riya replied. "I made breakfast if you're hungry."

"You know I am. It smells great, what's the occasion?" I asked.

Riya shrugged and traced a finger along the rim of his mug. Silently he stared down into the java abyss. "I just wanted to say I'm sorry about last night."

"Riya, we've talked about this. You have nothing to apologize for." I wondered if the conversation about meeting with that handler was what triggered his nightmare. If so, I wouldn't bother to call Artesia back. "We don't ever have to go back to that club again. It breaks my heart to see you upset. I just want you to be happy, Riya. That's all that matters to me."

"I know, but I feel bad for keeping you up," Riya replied.

"Riya, I know we don't have a traditional relationship, but we do have a relationship and I'm in this with you forever. I know I've told you that like a million times, I'm not going to leave you and I'm not going to let anybody hurt you again. I don't know what it's gonna take for you to believe me." No coffee, sad boyfriend, hate for the world that made him this way—all things that did not kick a day off to a good start.

"I believe you. The problem is my subconscious is fixated on past abuse and has trouble getting over it. You're the only person in the world I trust, Stefan. The only person in the world I love. The only person in the world who's ever loved me back," he admitted and though I already knew this, it still broke my fucking heart to hear it.

"I think we've done enough for me," Riya said. "Now, I think it's time we do something for you, Stefan. We can meet with that handler. I want to...I want to," he stumbled over his words. "I wanna try. For you and for us. It's been a long time since that happened, and I need to get over it."

"Riya," I got out of bed and crossed to where he sat and crouched down in front of him. "Riya, look at me." His sad little face turned my way. "Everyone heals in their own way and at their own pace. No one lived through what you did and no one, not even you, should try to convince yourself otherwise. You will get past this, and I'll be right by your side. If at any point you're uncomfortable with this handler or anything that he wants to do, you say the word and we stop, and I mean it for real and you know that."

"I do. I love you, Stefan," he leaned forward and wrapped his arms around my neck, hugging me tight.

"I love you, too, my little kitten."

After breakfast we finished our chores then I went outside to call Artesia.

"Good morning, Stefan. How are you?" she greeted me.

"I'm good. Could you maybe tell me a little bit more about that handler you mentioned?" I asked as my stomach churned. Was I doing the right thing? The right thing for us, that is, or was this all for me? I'd wanted a Daddy, or at least wanted to explore that option. One that would take care of us, make sure we ate and had toys—the whole package. No one had ever really taken care of Riya or me.

"Absolutely," she didn't hesitate with her response. "He's been a member of the club for more than a decade. He's had many boys, though not at the same time," she laughed. "But he's worked with some that other Daddies found too difficult and helped them overcome their challenges and move onto healthy partnerships. He's a very well-known handler and if I didn't think he was a good fit for the two of you, I wouldn't have bothered calling. Look, I know it's none of my business but if something happened to you guys at another club, I hope when you're ready you'll trust me enough to share your story with me and give me the opportunity to make it right. In this line of work, we owners frequently talk, and we take care of our own."

"What makes you think something happened to us?" How was this possible? This woman hardly knew us and yet she wanted to help. This sounded too good to be true.

"I have been in this business a long time, love, and I have seen the faces of many whose paths have crossed with those not worthy of the title of Dom or Mistress.

Safety is number one at my club. This is my life and I live the lifestyle. I've spent many long hours ensuring we have a safe, friendly environment and I won't tolerate any members being hurt—that's non-negotiable. The BDSM lifestyle gets a bad rap by those who don't take the time to learn about it. It's meant to heal, not hurt and if someone has violated the rules or taken advantage of another, I want the opportunity to eradicate it. I know you're new and neither of you know me, yet, but you'll soon find out I'm a no-nonsense woman and I care with my whole heart. Trust me, word gets around in this business, and we have ways of dealing with those who've stepped out of line. Please just keep that in mind," Artesia's voice left no room for questioning.

"Okay." I didn't know what else to say since it wasn't me who was the one that got hurt and I didn't want to speak for Riya in this case. This wasn't a circumstance where I needed to, this time it was up to him to share his truth. And I hoped he would, that would be the start to his healing process. At least, from what I read it was. He needed to trust the right person and open up to them. Maybe that was Artesia.

"On that note," Artesia began again, "what do your schedules look like? He owns his own business so he can make most days and times work. Given the club usually opens around eight pm, I'd be willing to open at six or even from four to six if that works better for you guys to meet. I would recommend for your first meeting you don't bring your gear. Sit and talk, get to know one another and see if this is even something you're interested in. First impressions say a lot with a handler or a potential Daddy. Feel them out, ask all the questions that you have. He's an open book and like I said, a very nice man and I'm proud that he's a member of our club and community."

"Well, Riya and I are both off today. Is that too soon?" I asked her, nervously chewing on my cuticles.

"Let me reach out to him and I'll call you back, all right?" she said.

"Artesia?"

"Yes, Stefan?"

"Thank you for giving us a chance to prove we're not who everybody thinks we are." Something in her voice told me this just may work out for us this time.

"You are very welcome. We'll talk soon." She ended the call. I stared out at the parking lot and gathered my thoughts before going inside. This was a lot to take in and while there really wasn't much to say to Riya, not at least until I knew the time was agreed upon, his reaction weighed heavily on me. When I finally went back in, he was curled up against the pillows on the bed and blankly stared at the television. I wasn't even sure he knew it was on.

Chapter Three

Riya

Based upon the look on Stefan's face, there was no doubt in my mind that we were moving forward with this. Stefan reiterated what Artesia said and that a meeting with this alleged handler was set up—for today. I was nervous as fuck. Many so-called handlers talked a good game but very few stayed true to their words. I wasn't a fan of humans in general, I hadn't found one outside of Stefan I could trust. And I must've really trusted him, or I wouldn't be sitting beside him on the bus headed downtown to a closed club.

Stefan took my hand in his, my heartrate immediately calmed. “Riya, it’ll be all right. You’ll see. If this guy wasn’t on the up and up Artesia wouldn’t have recommended him.”

Deep down, I knew he was right, but a haunting past never strayed far from the mind’s eye.

The parking lot was of course empty, we walked up to the front and Stefan knocked on the oversized door. I swear it echoed like a crypt door would. One of the beefy security guards answered the door. His stoic, overpowering presence was unnerving. I gulped and backed up without uttering a single word, though Stefan still firmly held my hand so I couldn’t make a break for it.

“Oh, um, hello,” Stefan nervously rambled. “We’re Stefan and Riya and we’re here to see Artesia.” The man said nothing but backed up and let us pass. Artesia appeared a few moments later.

“Good afternoon, gentlemen. I'm glad you could make it on such short notice. Please,” she gestured toward the waiting room furniture, “have a seat. Let's chat for a moment before he gets here.”

Stefan and I sat so close we shared a cushion. “Please don't be nervous. I'll be there through the initial introductions and if you wish for me to stay through the entire session I will. Though I can assure you this man is as genuine as I said. He does a lot for the community through altruistic measures such as donations, he’s headed up fundraisers, you name it—he does a lot for the LGBT community as well. As for this club, his company completed our last remodel." Artesia gestured around the room. This place was exquisite, no expense was spared. She ran a tight club and a very clean one at that. I only hoped we would get to stay this time, though we'd have to make payment arrangements in order to fund the high membership fees.

"We were only granted three passes when we signed up and we used them all. Do we have to pay for that?" Stefan asked. I hadn't even thought about that but then again, I always relied on Stefan to speak for both of us.

"No, consider this one on the house," Artesia smiled. I liked her, there was something real and warm about her.

"And if things go well, I'll likely add you to my membership," a deep voice sounded from behind us that sent chills running down my spine. Both Stefan and my gazes darted his way.

"It's you," Stefan whispered from beside me though everybody heard. When had he met this man?

"Yes, little pup, it's me. I was intrigued watching the two of you the other day and while I don't condone violence of any sort, including an attempt to bite another handler's hand, I can't say I didn't growl at him myself," he winked and holy shit, every hair on my body stood on end.

"Yes, I too agree with Jonovan. Stefan, Riya," Artesia pointed to each of us, "meet Jonovan Duarte." We both stood as if commanded as Jonovan crossed the room and shook our hands. I was mesmerized, unable to utter a single word. Not that I normally did in the presence of strangers. How I managed to do my daily job was beyond me. Maybe because it was a different persona. On the clock I was salesman Riya, after hours, not so much.

"Thank you, Artesia, for setting this up. I appreciate you doing so and the confidentiality regarding the members' personal information spoke highly of your character," Jonovan complimented her.

"Absolutely. The privacy and protection of my members is first and foremost. Would you gentlemen like to meet out here in the lobby, or just inside the club in the general gathering area? Or would you feel more comfortable in the play area?" Artesia asked us.

"Stefan, Riya?" Jonovan said. "Where would you be most comfortable?"

Stefan glanced at me, and I shrugged. This was gonna go however it was gonna go no matter where we sat. That was totally irrelevant, at least where we were now, we were strategically located next to the exit door if we needed to make a fast getaway. No, I take that back. I didn't believe that would be necessary. Something about Jonovan's presence spoke to me and even though he had not said much I could feel he was a protector. I only hoped he had no dark secrets that would jump out of the closet later and bite us.

"I'm good with here if you guys are?" Jonovan said.

Stefan was nervous. This was a side of him I didn't often see. He kept wiping the palms of his hands on his jeans. "Yeah, here's good, right, Riya?" I nodded and watched as Jonovan crossed the room and took a seat in the chair beside the couch, then turned to face us.

"I'm sure Artesia has filled you in, but again, I'm Jonovan Duarte. I've been a handler for many pups, kittens, a couple of ponies, and various animals. I even had a ferret once." He smiled, and I felt myself smiling back. "I've been in the pet play genre, gosh, for as long as I can remember. I want to say probably going on fifteen or sixteen years, and I've been a member of the Blue Underground since Artesia opened the club. I have no preference or favorite kind of pet. I love them all equally. I've had good boys, naughty boys, you name it, and even when the training or relationship ended, we always parted amicably. I've remained in contact with all of them, though many have moved on with their own Daddies. Some have even married, and I wish them well."

"We're gay, is that gonna be a problem?" Stefan blurted out. I jumped at his words not only for the way he said them but the decibel level for which he used.

Jonovan laughed. "No, I too am gay and do not see that as a problem, Stefan." Stefan visibly relaxed beside me. "Why don't the two of you tell me how you got into pet play? I don't want to be an ageist, but you do seem rather young, and I need to get a feel for what your expectations are. Do you use it as a means to unwind? Basically, what does pet play mean to you?"

"Well," Stefan began, "it was kind of accidental. I was watching silly animal videos on YouTube and a pet play one came up. There was a grown man in a leather mask wearing tiny leather shorts with a tail sticking out of them. He ran around chasing a ball another man threw for him. Craziest thing I ever saw, grown-ups acting like animals, and I showed it to Riya, and we laughed. Then we found ourselves diving deep down into that wormhole and watching every video we could find. Before long we figured what the heck, dropped down on all fours and ran around our apartment barking and meowing, playing without using our hands, and actually found it soothing. It was just kind of fun not to do anything, not to have to think, not to have to pay a bill, not to adult. We got to be silly and roll around on the floor with each other and one thing led to another and here we are. We started going to clubs about two years ago and we've been together for five years now."

"Six," seemed I found my voice. Jonovan nodded and smiled sweetly at me.

"Yes, sorry, six years," Stefan corrected.

"What dynamic are you two looking for? A handler? I assume based upon your last response you are boyfriends?" Jonovan asked.

"We're boyfriends but to be honest, something's missing. No, I'm not saying we're looking for you to be our Daddy, but we love each other and it's really kind of hard to build a relationship when you're both bottoms," Stefan admitted. Jonovan released a hearty laugh and the smile returned to my face. Not a regular occurrence in my world.

"My dear boys, please, I am not laughing at you, but I completely understand your predicament and you are correct—two bottoms or two tops do not complete a relationship. I would love the opportunity to work with you and if for some reason this does progress past the handler status, and we collectively decide we want more—which you would both have to agree upon. I want to make that clear. I do understand that Stefan speaks for Riya, but I do require both to speak up for themselves. No one's thoughts or feelings should ever be discounted and no two pets, no two people, no two anything are ever alike and need to be treated as individuals with their own thoughts and feelings," Jonovan said in a Daddy-Dom voice that had me quivering. Who was I and what had I done with Riya? I didn't respond to others that way. Ever.

Everything he said was perfect and though I'd heard similar words in the past, such as no means no, you say stop and it's over, we know how well that went. Honestly, it wasn't that long ago and that was our first club experience purely by accident. It was one of Stefan's infamous *we need a Daddy* ads in a paper that it should have never been put in. Answered by a man that never should have responded. He wasn't a Dom or a Daddy, he was an evil dick.

"Any other things within the BDSM realm you want to explore or kinks you'd like to share with me?" Jonovan asked.

Stefan again glanced at me, and my gaze instantly dropped. I was sure we both recalled that night and even though Stefan wasn't in the room when Dominic did what he did to me, I had shared some of it with him. But not all. I couldn't bring myself to say the words. Kink was a hard limit for me. No toys or weapons and absolutely no restraints. I had to be able to get away if I needed to.

"Riya doesn't care for any BDSM at all, he just likes to be a kitten," Stefan responded for me, and I was thankful he had.

"Duly noted," Jonovan replied, "and for you, Stefan?"

"I like being spanked. I think I'd like to be blindfolded and restrained. There are other things I'd like to try with the right person," Stefan admitted. He'd always been the more adventurous of the two of us but then again, I still wore the scars from my first dose of the lifestyle, and it wasn't by choice.

"Do you have a pet name when you play?" Jonovan asked us.

I shrugged. "We haven't played with anyone but each other so no one's ever asked that before."

"Thank you, Riya, for speaking up," Jonovan praised, and I sat up prouder. Hmm, maybe I did have a kink. Stefan had that in his ad but I didn't think anything of it until now.

"Kitty is fine for me, what about you, Stefan?" I asked.

"I'm good with Pup," Stefan replied.

"Pup and Kitty it is then. Does this mean the two of you will allow me to work with you and get to know you better?" Jonovan asked, and he seemed excited but then again, he was the one who reached out to us.

This time when Stefan looked at me, instead of my usual go to responses of nods and shrugs, I decided to adhere to Jonovan's earlier request and speak up. "For myself, I think I'd like that, but I have a lot of triggers."

"I'd like it, too, but is there some sort of form or contract we can fill out where we tell you more about what we do and don't like?" Stefan replied.

"Absolutely. I have a contract that I can e-mail Stefan and Riya and if Jonovan agrees, I can e-mail you his previously filled out form. Is that acceptable, Jonovan?" Artesia asked him.

"I think that would be great, then they can see all the kinks I enjoy outside of pet play. Please, don't be alarmed or overwhelmed when you read it. I'm a little more open than most, though none of it are a must or a deal breaker for me. I don't need them to make a relationship work, there are many kinks I've explored and enjoyed. I'm flexible but pet play is what I love, and I look forward to working with both of you. Are you comfortable exchanging phone numbers with me?" Jonovan asked.

"I think that's a good idea. Sometimes it's easier to text than talk, although I do understand the importance of certain conversations being had face to face," Stefan replied.

"Now that we've reached an agreement and will move forward with the sessions, would you prefer to have our first one here with others around or play in private?" Jonovan asked.

"I'm reluctant to say private," Stefan said, "just because of things that have happened in the past." He side-eyed me. "Maybe our first session should be here at the club with others around, even though I don't like being watched."

"Pet play and littles have their own special night on Wednesdays," Artesia reminded us, "and from eight to ten on Saturdays all the rooms are open but are quite busy. May I suggest a Wednesday night for your first session? I think it would be best."

"I think that's a great idea, Artesia," Jonovan agreed. "What do the two of you think?"

"We get our schedules on Sundays and since we are in retail, they change every week. But now that we've exchanged numbers, we can text you and let you know, if that's okay?" Stefan asked.

"That works fine for me. My schedule is generally flexible so I can make nearly any date and time work. I'd like to thank the two of you for allowing me this opportunity. It will be fun, and I look forward to playing with you," Jonovan told us.

Chapter Four

Jonovan

Why was I nervous?

I'd been doing this for a long time, training pets, and had been properly schooled by some of the best in the industry. I've had many pups of my own but what was it about working with these two that had me on edge, and not necessarily in a bad way? "You're being silly, Jonovan," I scolded myself, grabbing my keys and heading out the door before I could overthink this and do something stupid. If I canceled, I'd only live to regret it.

In typical Jonovan fashion, I was once again getting ahead of myself. Showing up on the first day bearing gifts may be a bit much for them. I assumed based on their gear the night I'd first seen them that they didn't have a lot of money. While I knew I wasn't their Daddy and I shouldn't point out their lack of proper gear, I still took it upon myself to buy them knee and paw pads. Even though they would be playing on a rubber mat tonight, they could still suffer injuries like rug burn when their skin met with the surface in the wrong way. I wasn't about to let them get hurt, not on my watch.

"Welcome, Jonovan," Artesia greeted me, and eyed the bag I had with a knowing smirk. "Your boys are in the changing room. Let me take you to them." We walked down the hall and as we neared the door that they were behind, Artesia turned to me. "I don't think I've ever seen you this nervous before. Is it nervous bad or nervous excited?"

"Definitely nervous excited. I just have a feeling, you know what I mean," I replied, not willing to give away too much.

"I do indeed. I'm interested to see how this goes for the three of you and I'll be watching. Have you considered becoming a full-time trainer here? The industry could use more like you, and I'd be honored to have you on staff," Artesia asked.

"I think once I took it on as a job it would take the fun out of it for me. Right now, it's more of a hobby, so to speak, though it's also a part of my lifestyle and I've missed having a pet, or in this case pets of my own," I honestly admitted. If all went well, I'd happily retire from training to tend to my own boys.

"I completely understand that," she smiled. "I'll leave you to it, but I'll pop into the playroom shortly and see how the play is progressing along."

"Thank you again, Artesia, for everything. I have a feeling these boys need me," I said, fiddling with the bag in hand. Why was I so out of sorts today?

"And you, likewise," Artesia winked before she sashayed away. I swear that woman had a sixth sense and knew what those who were lost sought. And she also knew how to help them get it.

When the boys came out of the changing room, they both jumped and shrieked as I approached them. "I'm so sorry, I didn't mean to scare you." I gave them a moment to catch their breath before I sprung the gifts on them. "Before we hit the play area, I wanted to give you this," I said and handed them the bag.

"What is it?" Stefan asked.

"It's a gift. I hope it wasn't too presumptuous or forward of me, these will help keep you safe and that's always number one. But I want you to have fun as well. Relax and enjoy yourself and you'll find that inner sense of peace you seek once you allow yourself to fully submerse into the therapeutic beauty of pet play." Fingers crossed I hadn't turned into the creepy old man after that lame speech.

"Thank you," Riya said. Stefan stared down at the bag as though he anticipated something would jump out of it.

"We'll be right back," Stefan said as he pushed Riya back inside the room. A few minutes later they emerged with the gear on. It was a proud moment for me, I loved it when my boys wore gifts I bestowed upon them. Some boys more than others only wanted lavish gifts while others felt bought. That was never my intention, making my boys happy in turn made me a happy Daddy.

"Excellent." They beamed at the words of praise. I guess this time my over exuberance was well played. "Shall we?" I gestured down the hallway toward the room and started to walk. The boys followed behind me.

A couple of handlers and their pets were already in there when we arrived. I was pleased to see that the guy the boys had the incident with last time wasn't here. At least not yet. I led them over to an unoccupied area we could use. "Okay, Pup and Kitty, let's start with some basic skills." They dropped down on all fours and trotted behind me toward the basket of toys. I pulled out a red ball for Pup, and a shiny fish-shaped toy for Kitty. Pup excitedly wagged his tail, tongue lolled to one side. "Are you ready to go, Pup?"

"*Ruff, ruff,*" he barked, his tush up in the air as he wiggled it back and forth and shook his tail. "Just a second, let me get Kitty set up with his toy." While Pup was ready and rearing to go, Kitty remained reluctant to follow suit.

As I walked toward Kitty, he cowered and shook. "Oh, my sweet little Kitten, I'll never hurt you. I don't know who made you feel this way but when I find them, they will regret it." Pup growled from behind me. "It's all right, Pup, I'm not gonna hurt your Kitty. I'll never hurt either of you." I held my hand out for Kitty to smell, timidly he sniffed it and pulled back. And then sniffed it again and stared up at me, eyes wide. He was curious as to how the stranger would treat him. "May I pet you, Kitty?" Pup still protectively growled though it had lessened. He needed to see I wouldn't hurt his Kitty as much as Kitty did. "It's okay, Kitty." Kitty's nose jutted forward as he sniffed my hand, a bit longer this time, so we were making progress. Slowly, I reached up and slid my hand along his spine. He arched his back as I stroked him a few more times. "There, there, sweet Kitty. See, I won't hurt you. Would you like to play with this shiny fishy?" Kitty reached up and swatted the toy in my hand and knocked it free. "There you go, Kitty. Go get it." He pounced off, snagged the toy and somehow the tiny toy managed to flip him over. Then Kitty held it tightly between its front paws while his back legs tried to kick it away. I smiled, loving how freely Kitty now played.

"See, Pup, Kitty is just fine. Let's play fetch," I juggled the ball from hand to hand, Pup's eyes never left it.

"*Ruff, ruff*," he responded.

"Okay, boy, here you go." I threw the ball in the opposite direction of Kitty. Pup bounded off and retrieved it in his mouth and whipped his tail around. "All right, Pup, bring it back. Bring the ball back to me." He headed toward me and just as he reached me, he turned and ran in the opposite direction and started barking again with his tail wagging. "Silly Pup, that's chase, not fetch," I informed him. "Come on, today we're learning how to play fetch. Bring me the ball." Slowly Pup crept forward and when he got within arm's reach, he bounded off again. "You are full of silliness tonight, aren't you, boy? Come," I commanded, "bring the ball and drop it at my feet." Pup trotted over, dropped the ball, sat back on his haunches and stared expectantly at me until I tossed the ball again.

Pup eventually grew bored of fetch and dug his nose into the container of toys and tossed them all over the place. Meanwhile, I wandered over to spend some time with Kitty. As I approached, he again curled in on himself. "It's just me, Kitty. I'm not going to hurt you." I sat down a couple of feet away and waited to see what he'd do. He glanced at me a couple of times then slowly edged near me, creeping across the floor. Meanwhile, Pup paid us no mind. He'd torn every toy from the box. I hope he knew he'd clean those up when he was done. "Come on, Kitty,

I won't hurt you." He came close and nuzzled my hand with his nose. I lifted it and stroked his head, then down his back to his tail and he arched into me and purred.

"Good Kitty, that's a good boy. Thank you for trusting me, that means a lot," I praised as he curled up along my side and allowed me to continue to stroke him. Eventually, he nodded off and Pup trotted over with a bone and dropped it at my feet. He stared at me, then glanced at Kitty, then back at me. Quizzically, he cocked his head to the side. "I think our Kitty was tired, Pup. What do you think?" He barked once and Kitty jumped. "Well, Kitty's awake now. You two have had a busy day, are you ready to call it a night?" At that point, Pup had curled up on my other side. The soothing strokes, something I hadn't had for a while, were lulling me as well. I knew I missed having a pet, I just didn't realize to what extent until this very moment. Pet play wasn't only therapeutic for the pets themselves, but for a seasoned handler and Daddy like me, they were as well. Today only served to reassure me that I wanted them for my own, but their trust would not come easily. I would have to earn it and I'd do everything in my power to make that happen.

"I think it's time to call it a night. What do you think?" They barely moved, I loved how comfortable they were getting with me, but it was time to go. "Come on, you two. Let's get you changed." Reluctantly, they got up and trotted on all fours until we reached the entryway where they stood and followed me back down the hall to the changing room.

"Will you still be here after we get changed?" Stefan asked.

"Yes, of course, sweet boy. I'd like to take you to dinner if that's all right?" They looked at each other and bobbed their heads up and down. It reminded me of those crazy little toy dogs people used to have in the back windows of their cars. "Excellent, get changed and we'll head out. Do you have a car here?"

"No, we don't drive. We took the bus, although sometimes when we're here and it's late we'll Uber home, but usually we take city transportation," Stefan replied. The thought of those two on the bus late at night filled me with dread.

"Well then, if you'll allow me to, after dinner I'll drive you home, make sure you get there safely," I offered and nearly held my breath as I awaited their reply. This was too new for me to use my Daddy voice and leave no room for argument. When we reached that point, they'd understand it was done out of love and nothing more.

"Thank you," Stefan said before they disappeared inside the room. I turned to lean against the wall and people watch when a body ran into mine and wrapped its arms around me. Imagine my surprise to find Riya standing there. I wound my arms around him and pulled him tight.

"What was that for, sweet Kitty?" I asked.

"Thank you," Riya replied.

"For what?"

"Even if this is the only night you play with us, thank you for being nice." He pulled away and darted back inside, leaving me stunned and staring at the closed door.

Yep, these two were meant for me and I'd show those sweet boys that there was still a good Daddy in the world who could love them like they'd never been loved before.

With them safely buckled in, I pulled out of the parking lot and headed toward my favorite late-night restaurant. Hell, my favorite restaurant period. Though in theory it wasn't too much after the dinner rush, so I hoped it wasn't too crowded. Stefan and Riya's curious gazes roamed the inside of my Ford F-150. She may not have been fresh off the lot, but I took good care of my baby girl and she still looked brand new.

The original truck I started the business with, my dad's old beater he gave me when I turned sixteen, we still used once in a while to haul lumber and whatnot, though for most of the projects we had materials drop shipped directly to site and the mobile techs had vans of their own. I still caught a glimpse of the old girl from time-to-time. It was fun to reminisce and recall how it all began and how far the business had come. Now, I'd reached the time in my life when I was ready to settle down, maybe not have a family per se, as in children, but a family that suited me and the man or men that would be a part of it.

"Here we are," I said as I pulled into the parking lot of my favorite pizzeria. The boys got out and followed me inside, normally being the Daddy that I am I'd insist they wait for me to open the doors, but we weren't there yet, and I didn't want to scare them away.

"Good evening, Jonovan," the hostess greeted us.

"How are you, Mariana?" I returned. She worked most nights because she was married to the owner's son. "You're looking beautiful as ever. If we could get a booth with a bit of privacy that would be greatly appreciated."

She smiled and nodded. "Follow me, gentlemen." She handed us each a menu as we took our seats. "Your waitress will be right with you."

The boys' gazes went from the menu, to each other, to me, then back to the menu. I figured they were mentally calculating how much dinner would cost. I may not be ready to push the Daddy scene on them yet, but I was ready to pay to feed them. "Pick whatever you'd like. Dinner is on me as a thank you for agreeing to let me be your handler."

Stefan sat straighter in his seat. "You don't need to do that." I fully expected him to protest.

"No, I don't, but I want to. Please, enjoy a meal on me." Reluctantly they agreed and their gazes dropped back down to the menu. I already knew what I wanted, being a creature of habit and though I had branched out and tried different dishes here, I always went back to my old standby. “I can personally tell you I’ve tried many things on this menu, though I generally order the same thing. I can assure you everything I've tasted has been nothing short of a culinary masterpiece.”

“You say the kindest things,” Sergio, the owner and head chef, said as he appeared beside our table.

“Good evening, Sergio, how are you doing?” I asked. It was always a pleasure to speak with him. The man was brilliant in the kitchen. My company had done some work here as well as at his residence.

“I'm doing fine now, Jonovan. Welcome back to our fine establishment, and who are your friends?” He nodded toward the boys.

“This is Stefan and Riya,” I introduced them, and purposely omitted how we met. I didn’t keep my lifestyle a secret by any means, but I wasn’t about to *out* them to the world.

“Nice to meet you both. Riya, that's a unique name,” Sergio said.

“I'm not sure where it came from but it's definitely hard when you want to find something personalized on a shelf in a store,” Riya replied. I think that was the most he’d spoken all night.

Sergio laughed. “I’m sure it is, but unique is never a bad thing, remember that. I'll leave you gentlemen to your evening. Enjoy,” Sergio said before he walked off.

"Wow, you must spend a lot of money here to have the owner come and talk to you," Stefan commented and immediately slapped a hand over his mouth. "Oh my God, I'm so sorry, that sounded rude and I didn't mean it that way."

I chuckled. "It wasn't taken as such but yes, I'm a single man who can cook yet chooses not to, so I end up eating here a couple of times a month and have been for years. Which brings my next question, if you don't mind me asking, how old are you?"

"Twenty-four," they said in unison. My first thought was *I have socks older than them* which I hoped wasn't true, and it had me mentally inventorying that dresser drawer. Reverse ageism wasn't good though the metaphor still stood.

"How old are you?" Riya surprised me by asking. Seemed the sweet kitty had an inquisitive side.

"I'm thirty-eight," I replied, waiting for their eyes to widen and pop out of their heads at our age difference. But it never happened, and they continued with the Q&A until the waitress came to take our orders. The boys each ordered a different dish, and I visualized the scene from *Lady and the Tramp* playing out in front of me as they shared their pasta. Well, as close as it would have come eating out of two bowls rather than one like the puppies in the movie did. Still, it was an adorable image just the same. I ordered the lasagna and made a mental note to ride the exercise bike double time later to work off the carbs, though it was more than worth it.

Things quieted once the salads and bread arrived, the boys dug right in. Between bites, I asked more questions just to get a feel for where they saw this going. "Would you like to play together again? With me I mean? Obviously, you play with each other," I rambled, not the norm for me. Generally, people didn't fluster me and I sure as hell didn't stutter or babble like an idiot.

They grinned and nodded and then Stefan replied, "We'd like that. Most Saturday nights we work, which is probably why we haven't run into you before, so we usually only go on Wednesdays. Well, for the two times that we went I should say. Would Artesia really let us keep going as your guests?'

"She absolutely will. Artesia is a natural nurturer, and she loves helping others come out of their proverbial shell and find their peaceful Zen. It's crucial for one to find a safe, healthy outlet to release stress and worries before it eats you alive. Whether it be in the form of BDSM, or a kink such as pet play or being a little. Hell, for that matter painting, ceramics, whatever outlet works for that person. All I know is it's unhealthy to keep it all pent up inside, everyone needs their happy place to survive," I replied. Probably shared more than they cared to hear but these were important things they should learn at their ages. It would serve to help them tremendously down the road.

"Makes sense," Stefan said, "but unfortunately because our schedules vary, we'd have to wait until Sunday each week to set our play dates for the following week."

"Once you get comfortable with me the option of playing at my house will be there. I'm not opposed to that, but I'll leave it for the two of you to decide if or when you reach that point. Either way, just let me know and we can make the necessary arrangements." I much preferred playing in the privacy of my home, less distractions for sure, but they had to be willing to make that first step.

"Thank you," they replied. That was the second time they spoke in unison. I began to think they shared a brain. I had to say even though they were young, I was jealous of the connection they had, the close bond and ability to know what the other thought and finish their sentences. Would I ever find that for myself?

Chapter Five

Stefan

A week had passed since we first played with Jonovan. The three of us texted off and on in the group chat we'd set up. He asked about things that we liked and disliked and although we'd grown comfortable enough with him to schedule a second session, we opted to meet at the club again on Wednesday night instead of at his home. Jonovan insisted on picking us up as opposed to our usual mode of travel, he wasn't fond of us on the bus at night. Riya and I had taken care of ourselves for so long it was hard for us to accept assistance from anyone and not fear there was an ulterior motive behind it. But Jonovan was easy to talk to and clearly enjoyed taking care of his...students? Not sure what the correct terminology was for a handler and those they trained. In the short while since we'd met Jonovan, he'd grown on me, and Riya clearly felt the same considering the fact he was so open with him.

"Hello, boys," Jonovan said as he got out of the truck and grabbed our bag. He tossed it in the back seat and hugged us both. His nice, warm, friendly hugs were addictive. When one was over, I was ready to line up for another. They were brief, though if we played our cards right maybe sometime soon...

Unrequited wishes from a lonely pup.

Sounded like the title to a story.

Hmm, maybe it could be mine and Riya's someday that included a happy ending.

"Hey, Jonovan. Thank you for picking us up," I said as soon as we took off down the road.

"It's not a problem at all. Don't think anything of it," Jonovan replied. "I know we texted, but I'd like to hear firsthand how your week was."

Riya blew a raspberry from the back seat, both Jonovan and I cracked up. "Oh, the peanut gallery is awake back there, I see," Jonovan smiled at him through the rearview mirror.

"It was boring," Riya complained.

"If you could do any job in the world, Riya, what would it be?" Jonovan asked him.

"Great question and honestly not one I ever thought about. I guess I'd just accepted the fact I'd have to work until I died, and it would be at a menial job because that's all I was good for. When you get told you're worthless all your life and you'll never amount to anything, you tend to believe it," Riya admitted while he stared down and twisted his hands in his lap. I couldn't believe he shared that much. Outside of me he never talked to a single soul about personal stuff.

"I can assure you just from the short time I've known you both that none of that is true. You're worth more than you know, Riya, and I'm certain you can do anything you set your mind to. What if I gave you a goal, so to speak? Think about the one thing in the world you like most and what it would take to be able to have that as your dream job and next time we get together, you tell me what it is. Deal?" Jonovan asked, making eye contact with him.

Riya sighed. "Okay, but I can't guarantee I'll come up with anything."

"That's all I can ask. What about you, Stefan?" He turned the question on me.

"Riya and I have similar stories, though in my house they lived and breathed sports. My dad wanted football players and he got one in my brother, then seven years later Mom had me. I was the child no one expected nor wanted and as you can see, I'm not built for any kind of sports. As soon as I turned eighteen, he told me to get out and find my way in the world. I never measured up for him even with straight As. That was the last time we spoke, and Mom wasn't the motherly type, so I've not heard a peep from her either. I've never focused on any one thing outside of surviving, but I guess if I thought long and hard about it, I would probably do something with animals in some capacity, even though I never had a pet of my own. Huh, seems ironic pet play was my chosen outlet."

"Maybe not so ironic after all," Jonovan winked. "All right, enough of this depressing shit. You guys think about that question long and hard and the next time we get together I'd like to hear what you've come up with." We both groaned. "How about a bit more enthusiasm here, boys?"

"Does it come with dinner?" Riya asked, showing his smart-ass side.

"Wow, someone found their voice and just came barreling out of the door with it, didn't they?" Jonovan teased and was all smiles. I thought he enjoyed this as much as we did. "But to answer your question, yes, it comes with dinner. I need to feed my boys after all."

His boys.

Was that the role we wanted, Riya and I? I didn't have to think too long on that. Riya and I enjoyed our time with Jonovan and the connection was undeniable. His presence exuded safety, and caring. Like he protected those he cared about and not in an overbearing way. And the way Riya took to him said a lot. He was never like this outside of the apartment and was really excited about tonight. Could I see us with Jonovan, as his pets? I could, though I didn't want to get too far ahead of myself and risk heartbreak. Was Jonovan even interested in us as in dating or only in being our trainer? Maybe when he called us his boys, he meant it from a handler standpoint and not as a boyfriend. I don't know, maybe I was just wishful Jonov-ing.

When we arrived at the club tonight, Artesia was speaking with one of the other handlers as they walked down the hall toward the pet play area. Riya and I went into the changing room we were assigned and slipped into our gear and then followed Jonovan out onto the mats. We had just got set up with our toys when something spooked Riya and he reverted into the terrified, shivering person he was during his nightmares.

"My sweet Kitten, what's wrong?" Jonovan crouched in front of Riya and asked him. When he reached out to stroke Riya's back, Riya scrambled into the corner of the room.

"Riya, what's going on?" I asked, though it seemed the wrong thing to do as his tears increased and he jumped into my arms.

"Stefan?" Jonovan questioned, his face awash with sympathy and concern for Riya.

"Kitty, what's happened? Who hurt you?" Jonovan asked.

"D-D-Dominic," Riya stuttered.

"Dominic?" Jonovan questioned, clearly confused.

"Dominic isn't here, Riya." He'd never reacted this way while away, but his gaze remained pinned to the windows. I followed his line of sight and saw the man himself. "Dominic Richards." I growled. Artesia and Jonovan turned toward the windows and there he stood, cocky as ever.

"Riya, did something happen between you and Dominic?" Artesia asked him. She'd come over during the commotion to check on us.

It wasn't my story to tell but seeing that man again and Riya in this state, I couldn't take it. "Yeah, you can fucking say that," I growled. "'No means no' means nothing to Dominic and while I don't know the full extent of what he did to Riya, I do know enough to want to rip his fucking heart out." Jonovan snarled, fists clenched at his side and he turned to heard toward the door, but Artesia stopped him.

"Jonovan, let me handle this," she told him, then pressed her earpiece and began speaking so low we couldn't hear her.

"If he hurt my boys there will be nothing that can stand between me and him. He'll regret it, I'll see to it personally," Jonovan growled the words as I made a mental note to never piss him off. Wow, angry Jonovan was a force to be reckoned with. Was it wrong that his standing up for us turned me on?

That was twice now he'd called us his boys.

I didn't fear for Riya or me in the least, Jonovan was in protective Daddy mode and right then I knew I wanted him to be ours, new relationship or not. Artesia continued to speak into her earpiece and before Dominic or Jonovan could make a move toward each other, two of Artesia's guards flanked Dominic in the hallway. I didn't know what they said to him, but Dominic was clearly pissed and pointed in our direction. The guards restrained Dominic and escorted him away and as soon as he was out of sight, Riya went limp in my arms.

"Riya?" I shook him. "Riya?" I began to panic, in an instant Jonovan was beside us and scooped Riya into his arms.

"Oh, my sweet Kitty, he'll pay for whatever he did to you, mark my word." Jonovan rose with Riya as though his weight were nothing. "Come, Stefan. Let's get changed and go home." I nodded and followed, though I really did not want to go home. Dominic knew where we lived, and I hated that and although he left us alone after the last incident, I didn't think we'd get off as easily this time.

Jonovan carried Riya all the way back to the changing room. "Is he gonna be okay?" I asked as he laid him on the bench.

"He will be with us by his side, Pup. Does he pass out often?" Jonovan asked.

"No, this is the first time that I know of," I replied.

"Whatever he did to our Riya, it must've been bad to cause this kind of a response. We will get to the bottom of this, I promise you, Pup," he said sweetly to me. I knew without a doubt his words were true and he'd handle it, I just hoped he didn't do anything to land himself in jail. I hurried and changed out of my gear while Jonovan changed Riya. Just as he'd finished, Riya came around.

"Sweet, sweet Kitty," Jonovan said, brushing Riya's curls aside. "Are you all right?" Riya glanced around the changing room and then down at himself. "I hope it's okay that I changed you out of your gear. Stefan was here the entire time."

Riya looked up at me and asked, "Is he...is he gone?" When I nodded, he visibly relaxed.

"Let's get you home and fed," Jonovan said.

"I don't wanna go home, he knows where we live," Riya nearly screamed, fear took control and pushed aside any calm he previously felt.

"My sweet little Kitty, I had no plans of letting you go home tonight. Are you both off tomorrow?" he asked us.

"Yes," I replied.

"Then I'd like to take you to my house, if that's all right with both of you? I feel the need to hold my boys tonight." Though Jonovan asked it, I got the feeling *no* wasn't a viable answer and not in a bad way. He was determined to keep us safe.

"Okay," Riya squeaked out.

"You boys stay here and keep the door locked. I'll be back in a moment. Don't let anyone but Artesia or me in, understood?" We bobbed our heads and then Jonovan kissed the tops of our heads, internally it sent me into a head over heels spiral. As soon as the door closed, I moved to the bench beside Riya and hugged him to me while we waited for Jonovan's return. Though he was only gone a few minutes, it felt like forever to us.

"Yes?" I answered when the knock came.

"It's me, sweet Pup," Jonovan's voice returned.

I walked over and let him in. "Are you all right to walk right now, Riya, or would you like for me to carry you?" Jonovan asked him.

"I can walk, but thank you," Riya blushed.

I gathered our stuff in the tote bag which Jonovan took from me to carry. With a protective arm around each of us, he pulled us against his sides. "Don't worry, boys, he's gone, and he's not allowed back. But unfortunately," he paused, "that will require a deposition from the two of you about what happened."

Riya's terror-stricken eyes filled to the brim with tears. "I don't want Riya to hurt anymore," I replied.

"I don't either, but I also don't want that man to be allowed to hurt another and if he comes near either one of you, there will be hell to pay," Jonovan's voice hit a deep, dark note and I knew he meant business.

There was no mistaking the meaning behind those words—Jonovan would protect us.

Chapter Six

Riya

The ride to Jonovan's house was silent and it was all my fault. Had I been able to better protect myself and not be such a wuss, none of this would've happened. Was Jonovan mad at me? Would he punish me? I hoped not, things between us were going so well, comfortable even, and I didn't want to fuck it up. Stefan always wanted a Daddy, and this was important to him, but now I too found myself wanting a Daddy and his name was Jonovan.

"I know that look on your face, Riya. Don't you dare." Stefan warned me as soon as we stepped inside Jonovan's house. A beautiful fawn Boxer came running toward us wiggling its nubby tail and pranced so excitedly it nearly folded itself in half.

"Oh my God! Puppy, puppy, puppy," I chanted and dropped down to hug him. His tongue covered my face and Stefan's as we rolled around with him. It was amazing how quickly all the bad things in the world went away and all it took was this beautiful Boxer. "What's its name?"

"This is my boy, Titus. Titus, meet Stefan and Riya," Jonovan introduced us.

"Titus, what a great name," Stefan said as I broke into a fit of giggles as Titus's tongue bathed my face. I couldn't help it since I was ticklish everywhere.

"Good thing he has a dog door and goes in and out or I'd be worried he'd piddle on the floor right now with as excited as he is," Jonovan said, smiling down at us. "Come, let me show you guys around." Stefan, Titus, and I followed Jonovan as he took us through the house. I hopped from side to side and Titus mimicked me as we made a game of it.

"As you can see from the front of house, it's an open floor plan. My team, my dad, and I gutted it. Talk about a fixer upper," he sighed, "this poor house had been through hell and back. Kitchen and living room are self-explanatory, and my office is over there," Jonovan pointed off to the far corner where an open door was. "Down this hallway are the bedrooms, a total of three, a guest bathroom, and in this room," he opened the door and sat our bag down, "is the master suite. You boys are welcome to sleep in here with me tonight, and I promise it's just to sleep and hold each other, or you're welcome to share one of the other rooms. I'll leave that decision up to you. In the meantime, make yourselves at home while I fix dinner. Do either of you have any food allergies I should be aware of?"

"I'm allergic to pumpkin," Stefan said.

"I don't think I'm allergic to anything," I replied. Jonovan's house was amazing and immaculate, but it was one of those houses where you weren't afraid to touch something for fear of getting a fingerprint on it. It was the opposite, warm and inviting, and I was ready to curl up on the couch with one of the big fluffy blankets he had on the back of it and fall asleep while petting Titus.

"Does Titus sleep with you?" Stefan asked.

"Yes, even though he has his own bed," Jonovan rolled his eyes.

"Then I want to sleep in your bed," I called out from the living room.

Jonovan laughed. "Oh, so the key to your heart is through my dog, duly noted. Make yourselves at home, boys. There is soda in the fridge, and I'll whip up a quick pasta dish for us." Stefan and I wandered around and found a dog bed and a basket of toys in the living room. Titus was just as curious about us as we were of him but once we got close to his toy stash, that little nub went wild.

"Titus, wanna play fetch?" Stefan asked. Titus answered with a bark. "Oh my God, that was too cute."

We played with Titus while Jonovan cooked. Whatever he was making smelled wonderful, and my tummy grumbled rather loudly. "I heard that!" Jonovan called from the kitchen. How he heard that over our laughter was insane. We had so much fun with Titus we lost track of time. "Ready to eat, boys?" Jonovan called out. "You, too, Titus." The three of us bounded into the kitchen, Titus wove in and out between Stefan and me. We had zero fears of falling, far too busy having more fun than we'd had in forever and had we landed on our butts it would've resulted in another round of uncontrollable giggles.

Jonovan filled Titus's food dish while Stefan and I washed up. When we returned from the bathroom the dining table was set. "Um, what's the green stuff?" Stefan asked.

"That's basil pesto, I always keep some in the freezer because it thaws quickly. And the other green bowl is salad. Please don't tell me you guys live off fast food?" Jonovan groaned.

"Maybe?" I question-asked. "We take turns cooking but it's pretty basic stuff." And cheap at that, but I didn't admit that aloud. Needless to say, when Ramen was on sale, we stocked up.

"Well, if you don't like it you don't have to eat it. I like to add chopped tomatoes and a bit of lemon to mine," Jonovan said, doing just that. Stefan and I did the same.

"Oh, that's not too bad," I took a second bite. "What did you call this?"

"Pesto. I'm glad you like it. What about you, Stefan?" Jonovan asked him but Stefan was too busy shoveling it in to manage a word. "Easy, Pup, or you'll choke." Stefan paused for the briefest of moments before he went right back to it.

I shook my head. "He likes it and he's the pickier one of us." I didn't remember anyone cooking for me, at least not since I was too young to work the stove, and it was likely the same for Stefan. As soon as Titus finished eating, he went outside and zoomed back in a few minutes later. "Someone has the zoomies," I smiled. Having a dog around was pure entertainment.

"Yes, he gets that way once he's empty. He'll be ready for round two of playtime here shortly," Jonovan said as he stood to clear the table.

"You cooked, the least we can do is clean," Stefan said, his bowl finally empty.

"While I appreciate that, part of being a Daddy is taking care of your boys and that includes cooking and the dishes," Jonovan replied.

"Well, twice you've called us your boys and now this third time you've mentioned taking care of your boys. So, you're either hiding another pair or..." Stefan trailed off, I'm sure regretting his outburst, but I too was curious as to what that meant.

"Why don't you two go and wear Titus out while I clean up and then we can talk. Deal?" Jonovan said. My gut clenched and I wondered if Stefan got too far ahead of the game. I hoped this wasn't over before it really had a chance to start. I wasn't ready to give up Jonovan or Titus now, for that matter. Stefan's shoulders slumped, and I knew he regretted asking. "No pouting, it's not what you think," Jonovan said. "Wait," he called out and we stopped. He dried his hands on a towel as he neared. "I can't take the sad puppy eyes from my Pup," Jonovan tilted Stefan's chin upward and kissed him first, then me. "Go play, I'll be in momentarily."

He kissed us.

Stefan stared off while his fingertips traced the outline of his lips. "Come on, lover boy," I nudged his shoulder with mine, "let's go play with Titus." Though I felt the same way, I wasn't as open with my emotions as Stefan was. I preferred to keep them bundled up inside, less chance of getting hurt...again.

It didn't take long as Stefan watched Titus play for him to join in and fall into his puppy headspace. I was extremely grateful he didn't pick up Titus's toys with his mouth because they were obviously well played with. Though he did manage to nudge the ball around with his nose.

Curiously, Titus tilted his head from side to side while he tried to figure out what the silly human was up to. Eventually he gave up and joined in while I pounced around. I didn't play with any toys but watching them put me in a silly mood and while I never fully fell into my kitty space, this was just enough to lighten the mood and make the night fun. When Jonovan's laughter rang out behind us all three heads whipped around to see his beautiful smile as he watched us play, he obviously enjoyed it as much as we had.

"Now, if this isn't a sight to see, two puppies and a kitty. Never would I have imagined I'd see this in my house, though I am hopeful it'll happen more often." He took a seat on the middle cushion of the couch. "All right, you two, let's have a chat while Titus gets water all over the floor with that crazy tongue of his." Stefan and I sat beside Jonovan and waited for him to start the conversation. We had no idea which way this would go but after that kiss the negative thoughts nearly evaporated, and I was hopeful. Jonovan wound his fingers through ours and kissed the knuckles. A sweet sentiment I'd never experienced, and it had my heart doing summersaults. "Stefan, Riya, I know this is new and I don't want to rush you boys, but I'd like to date you both."

Jonovan glanced at us, gauging our reactions. "Yes," Stefan bobbed his head up and down so fast I thought it might launch off his shoulders.

Jonovan then turned to me, "What about you, Riya? I don't want you to feel forced into anything because this one on the other side of me is over exuberant, but what would you like?"

I appreciated that Jonovan took my feelings into consideration and while I was nervous, I didn't have to think long about it. I wanted this just as much as Stefan did but again, back to that holding my emotions back thing I did. *Don't overthink it, Riya, live in the now.* "I'd like that, too, Jonovan."

"You two have made me a very happy Daddy and I think Titus will be thrilled to have the two of you around more. Now, to the sleeping arrangements. I know you don't have a change of clothes, but I have some T-shirts if you would like to wear them to sleep in," Jonovan offered.

"That will work. Thank you and thanks for dinner," Stefan replied.

"Yes, thank you," I said. "Dinner was great."

"I'm thrilled you both enjoyed it." Jonovan eyes darted over to Titus passed out on his dog bed snoring away. I guess when your snout was as smooshed up as his was you didn't have any choice, but he was far too cute to fuss at and I giggled. "Oh, you think it's funny now. Just wait until you hear that all night long. It takes some getting used to," Jonovan teased.

"Wait, don't you have to work tomorrow?" I asked him.

"My sweet Kitty, self-employment perks. I can work from home or not at all and for tomorrow I choose the latter. I'll fire off a text to my assistant and let her know I'm taking a day off. I have plans with my boys." He got up and headed down the hallway.

Stefan and I swooned, goofy smiles and heart-shaped cartoon eyes. I felt like we'd just won the lottery. We got a protective Daddy who could cook, and a new puppy to play with. The world had finally changed course in a positive way for us and I for one wasn't about to screw that up and I knew Stefan was of the same mindset.

It was slightly awkward, coming out of the bathroom in a shirt that wasn't mine, and then standing at the foot of a bed that wasn't ours. Like marionettes, we waited for the puppet master to pull our strings. Only we were willing dolls in this scenario, not ones created for a single purpose but ones who hoped to be part of larger plans. Hopefully...

Hope had become the number one word in my vocabulary.

Titus was the first to jump up on the bed, then flipped around to stare at each of us. His tongue hung from the side of his mouth while his nubby tail wagged a mile a minute. "Well, Titus has chosen his side," Jonovan joked. "Did you boys want to sleep in here with me or in the guest room?"

"Here," Stefan answered before I could say a word, though the same one was locked and loaded, ready for me to shout.

"Riya?" Jonovan asked. I liked that he wanted both our responses, not just one. Already, he treated us as equals and with respect.

"Here," I allowed the word to come, and it felt so right. I crawled up the middle and Titus was all over me.

"I guess those two are settled in. Do you have a side preference, Stefan?" Jonovan asked.

"Not really," Stefan replied, as he headed to one side and Jonovan to the other. I just wanted to be held by them both which was why I selfishly chose the middle. Plus, the element of surprise kept them on their toes. This was the new and improved Riya, and he was going to live it up while he could.

"All right, Titus," Jonovan said as he reached over to shut off the light, "you may need to sleep in your own bed tonight."

Ruff!

"Oh, is that how it's going to be? No whining then when you can't spin fourteen times to find just the right spot."

Ruff!

With the light off, Titus did just that—spun several times but in the end he hopped off the bed. I guess there were too many bodies in the way.

Stefan snuggled up to me, his arm wrapped around my waist. “Goodnight, Riya. Love you,” he said with a kiss.

“Night Stefan, love you, too.” We never went to bed without saying it. A simple promise we made when we stepped outside of the friendship zone. We’d not always been exclusive, though the last two years we had been. Jonovan would be our first since and if all went well, our forever, but I didn’t want to get too excited because life always had a way of bursting my bubble.

Chapter Seven

Jonovan

What was the protocol? Did I roll over and kiss them both then cuddle up to Riya? Was that over stepping? *Okay, Jonovan, you're the Daddy here and you are way overthinking this.* Remember the golden rule—communication.

"Boys, can Daddy have a kiss, too?" I sprung the title I longed to hear come from them.

"Yes, please." As expected, Stefan was the first to reply, though I was surprised when Riya claimed the middle position. Stefan leaned over and pressed his lips to mine. How I wished the light was still on, to see their fluttering lashes as our lips parted. A slight blush to their cheeks with a hint of a smile and to know I was the one that put it there.

"Goodnight, sweet Pup," I said as he lay back.

Riya threw his leg over mine and claimed my lips in a fierce, possessive kiss. It took me by surprise and took a moment to get my bearings as I'd only expected a simple peck. When his tongue slid along the seam, I gasped, which forced my lips apart and he dove right in. Oh, this sweet, shy, yet brazen kitty would surely keep me on my toes. Though when things quickly heated up to a point I knew we weren't prepared for, I had to put the brakes on.

"Sweet boy, you're showing your impish side," I warned, more to myself than him. I was ready to flip him over and claim him and while my cock was ready and willing, I knew my boys weren't.

"Sorry," Riya apologized though his tone was anything but apologetic.

"I couldn't see it, but it sure sounded hot," Stefan said.

"Yes, er, um," I muttered, mentally commanding my dick to stand down. "As much as I loved it, I'm not sure the three of us are prepared for that next step." Sometimes being the one in control sucked. "Goodnight, boys."

"Night," they said in unison. Riya kept his leg wrapped around mine, his head on my chest and Stefan's hand was on Riya's hip. This was nothing short of perfect.

This right here was the life I wanted. Did I ever see myself in a poly relationship? No, not really. Sure, I'd had threesomes before, though none of which I desired for more than a one and done. A means to get off and agreed upon by all parties involved before it started. But this, this felt right. Content, and with a sappy grin, I fell asleep nestled up with my boys.

After sleeping far better than I'd anticipated given the extra heat in the bed, I woke the next morning to the lovely sound of giggles and a canine pup bouncing between bodies. "All right, boy, time to feed you."

"I could eat," Stefan said as he bounced in the opposite direction of Titus. I didn't know who the bigger puppy was, size wise it was obvious but mentally I think right now they were on an even level, but they were having a great time.

"Crazy pups, and my pretty Kitty, too, let's head to the kitchen for breakfast."

"Yay!" Stefan and Riya cheered. The pitter patter of dog claws and naked feet as they scrambled down the hardwood hallway was like music to my ears. This house had been empty and silent for far too long. With it being only Titus and me, I hadn't realized how lonely I truly was until there were other bodies here. Bodies that already brought me joy and happiness in such a short time and to Titus as well.

After I tended to the morning bathroom ritual, I met the boys in the kitchen. They were so busy horsing around they didn't hear me come in. When I threw a scoop of kibble into Titus's dish their heads popped up. "What can we do to help?" Riya asked.

"Why don't you two wash your hands and get the coffee started while I scramble the eggs and make omelets. Or better yet, why don't we put Stefan on coffee duty and Riya, you take the wheel and make the toast. Sound like a plan, guys?" I suggested.

"Yes," they replied and proceeded to open cupboards to locate the items they'd been tasked with. I could have helped them, but it was more fun watching them ransack my kitchen and find their way around it. I wanted them to feel at home and the best way to do that was to dive in and learn where everything was. Together we had breakfast on the table in twenty minutes flat. Riya had done a complete turnaround since we first met, and I was elated to have had a hand in drawing him from his shell. There was still a long way to go but at this rate we'd be there in no time.

Far too quickly the fun came to an end. Stefan sighed and tossed his napkin on the plate. "I hate to be the voice of reality, but we need to get home and do laundry before we go back to work tomorrow."

Riya was just as defeated as Stefan was. "I don't want to leave," he whispered.

"I don't want either of you to leave and I'm sure Titus feels the same." Collectively, we glanced at the furball curled up underneath the table patiently awaiting any errant scraps that may have found their way to him. "Text me your schedules and maybe we can plan another sleepover this weekend, okay?" I asked, though I was reluctant to let them go.

Somberly, we worked as a cohesive team and had the kitchen cleaned up in record time. The Daddy in me wanted to tell them to go sit while I did it, but I knew it was important to them to be a part of the chores, too. They wanted to feel useful and that was something I had to be able to accept and understand. I had learned so much about my boys in the last twenty-four hours and couldn't wait for what they had in store for me.

Stefan and Riya said their goodbyes to Titus and hopped in the truck. The drive to their apartment wasn't long but I hated the uncomfortable silence and that it saddened my boys we had to part, albeit temporarily. In the short time since we met, I'd reached the point where I knew I'd do anything for them. Within reason of course, sort of...who was I kidding? The draw to give them the world was scary and exciting. It's funny what a fine line there was between emotions.

Before long, we pulled up in front of the complex and I drove around to the back where their building was. Something was off and a quick glance up the stairs to their door confirmed my suspicions. "Boys, stay in the truck, please." Both their heads popped up and they followed my line of sight toward their apartment. Their jaws went slack, and they reached for the door handles. "Please, boys, trust me and stay in the truck with the doors locked."

I grabbed my phone as I slipped out and dialed 911.

"911, what's your emergency?" the operator asked.

"I'd like to report a break-in," I replied and quickly read off the address to her.

"Sir, please do not enter the premises. Wait for the authorities to arrive," she directed.

"Understood."

The police came faster than I had anticipated, generally something of this nature had them taking their sweet ass time getting to. Maybe today was an underwhelming day for them or they were nearby. As soon as they parked, I waved the boys over to where we stood.

"Gentlemen," one of the officers said as they approached us. "I'm Officer Dennison, this is Officer Thomas," he introduced them, "are you the ones that reported a break-in?"

"Yes, I did," I replied. "But these two are the ones that live there." The officers took down the boys' names and gathered any pertinent information they could from them.

"When was the last time you were home?" Officer Thomas asked.

"Yesterday. We left around four pm," Stefan said. Riya was far too emotional to speak, he hung onto Stefan like a life preserver.

“Please wait out here while we clear the premises,” Officer Dennison directed. Both officers went inside and re-emerged a few minutes later. “It’s clear. Would you gentlemen please come with us and let us know if anything is missing so we can add it to the report?”

The boys nodded but said nothing as they followed the officers inside while I remained on the landing outside the door. I had another phone call to make.

“This can’t be good,” Artesia said when she answered on the first ring.

“I think we've got a problem and I'm 99.9% certain I know who was behind this.” I filled her in on what had happened and that the boys were currently inside with the police surveying the damages.

“We share the same suspicion. I guess that answers the question as to whether he knew where they lived,” she sighed.

“I hadn’t had a chance to ask but should verify. I'm going to help pack them up and have them stay with me. Even if the landlord came today and replaced the door, I wouldn't feel safe leaving them here. Not until he’s behind bars,” I nearly growled the last few words.

“Agreed. Let me do some digging,” she said and then hung up. I headed in to talk to the police and see the damage for myself.

“Since nothing is missing, we’ll submit the report and email you a copy. In the meantime, I would recommend staying elsewhere, if at all possible," Officer Dennison told the boys as I walked in.

"Oh, it's possible," I replied. Both boys ran to me, and I wrapped my arms around them, not giving two shits whether or not these officers were homophobic. My boys needed me, and I'd be there come hell or high water. "Let's gather what we can and take it back to my house."

Their crestfallen features were nothing short of soul crushing. "We worked so hard for all of this," Stefan said. "It wasn't much but it was ours." Riya cried harder at his admission and I squeezed them tighter and pressed my lips to the tops of their heads.

"I'm so sorry, boys, but we will get to the bottom of this. I agree with the officers, I don't feel comfortable leaving you here," I admitted. Their heads nodded in agreement against my chest, neither released the death grip they had on me or each other.

"Sir," Officer Thomas said to me, "since they'll be staying with you, we need your name and phone number for the report in case we need to reach out."

"Absolutely." After I'd provided them with the necessary information, they left the boys and I to sort through their things. We grabbed a wad of grocery bags and loaded up what we could. It appeared our alleged perpetrator had an anger management issue. He sliced the bed pillows, the mattress, anything he could get his hands on which included most of their clothes, too. The TV was smashed, anything and everything he could get his hands on were destroyed. The thought of what could have happened had the boys been here... *No, you can't go down that path, Jonovan. You've got them, they're safe with you.*

Thank fuck for that.

"There's nothing worth saving," Stefan sighed and tossed down the handful of shredded fabric he had. "We'll need to go get new clothes. Who would do this? We had no enemies that I'm aware of."

Did I share my thoughts or even hint at the hunch I had? Before I could, Riya spoke up.

"Dominic."

"Stefan, why don't you call the landlord and tell them what happened. Feel free to let them know where you'll be staying and give them my phone number as well." He nodded and slid his phone from his pocket. In this instance, it was best to remove Riya from handling the situation. My sweet Kitty was the more fragile one, though I knew Stefan held on by a tattered thread.

"Come here, Kitten." As soon as he was in my arms, he lost it. "Sweet Kitty, I'm so sorry this happened. I promise, Daddy will make it better," I threw the term out again, hoping it would soon catch on. "We'll stop by the store on the way home and pick up everything you boys need."

"We-we," he stuttered between sobs, "we can't afford that."

"Sweetheart, Daddy didn't ask if you could. Please let me take care of you both," my heart stammered as I waited for an argument to ensue, one I wouldn't allow. Emotions were high and I only wanted my boys to breathe and not worry, though I knew they still would.

Riya glanced up at Stefan who must've given him the sign he was looking for. "Okay."

As we left, the superintendent arrived to secure the apartment. The few bags of belongings the boys salvaged were placed in the back seat. The intruder purposely left the refrigerator open, ensuring the food would rot and then tore through the cupboards and destroyed dishes and food staples alike. Clearly, the purpose was to leave them in need. Had he counted on them calling him to be their savior? Hoping to swoop in and save the day? Fucking bastard, I knew he was behind this.

During our shopping trip, Artesia called and confirmed my worst fears. "Jonovan?" she asked as an overhead announcement was read. "Where are you?"

"Sorry about that. Everything the boys owned was destroyed so I took them shopping to replace what we could," I informed her. "Please tell me you've got news?"

"I do, but you're not going to like it," she replied.

"Oh, I can guarantee that," I said. "Fill me in."

"Well, it started by reaching out to fellow club owners. Needless to say, he's been banned from all for quite some time and has been trolling Craigslist for his victims. Riya is one of many but deemed the one that got away. The rest he tortured until he was done with them and cast them aside," Artesia said.

"Mother fucker," I growled.

"It gets better. One call led to another which ended with me talking to the detectives who are currently investigating him. I mentioned what happened to Stefan and Riya's apartment today and they've now taken over the case, too. Jonovan," she paused.

"Why do I get the feeling I'm not going to like what you're about to ask of me?" I asked.

"Because you're not. The detectives would like to interview the boys tomorrow. I offered up the club as a neutral place but if you feel they'd be more comfortable somewhere else, they're willing to meet them there. While they couldn't provide many details, I was able to find out that several of his victims had been wounded severely enough it landed them in the hospital. This man is an abuser, not a Dom, though he parades around like he's an award-winning one. We've got to put a stop to this before he kills someone and right now his sights are set on Riya," Artesia said, though I wish she hadn't.

Chapter Eight

Stefan

I knew the moment I walked up to the cart that something was wrong. Jonovan was angry. Was it with us?

"Okay, I'll talk to them and get back with you," he said to whomever he was on the phone with before he hung up.

"Is everything all right?" I asked, fearful to put the items I held in the cart only to be embarrassed when he tossed them aside and walked away. Riya stood beside me with the same fear reflected in his eyes.

"No, but we can talk once we get home. Did you boys find everything you needed?" he asked and took the piles from our arms. I breathed a sigh of relief as he placed them in the cart. "Can you get work clothes here or should we go elsewhere for those?"

"Shoot, work," Riya's shoulders slumped. "How will we get there?"

"Kitten," Jonovan said, "let me take care of that."

Was this happening too fast? Were Riya and I finally in the right place at the right time even taking into consideration what just happened? I knew Riya was right, Dominic was behind this and without a doubt this was only the beginning of what he had in store for us. He was pissed that he was escorted out of the Blue Underground and hopefully he wouldn't find out where Jonovan lived and mess with us there or come to our work. I completely regretted ever letting him drive us home from the club and now we've lost everything. I hated him even more. The break-in was a warning, a way to tell us this battle had only just begun.

I took Riya outside while Jonovan paid for our stuff, it was best that neither of us saw the dollar amount. We'd be riddled with guilt we'd never get over. As soon as Jonovan exited, we followed him to the truck and helped load the bags. "Crap, we've got to work tonight," I said the thought aloud as it entered my head.

"Is there any possibility you could call out?" Jonovan asked us. I didn't feel that this was him trying to control us, but more like he was afraid to leave us alone and risk having something happen to us. I couldn't deny I felt the same way.

"I think he's right, Riya. We're not in the right state of mind to work tonight and there's no way either of us will be able to focus. Plus, we never call out so we have plenty of sick days to use," I added, knowing Riya's first thought would go to money.

"You're right," Riya agreed. On the way back to Jonovan's, Riya and I both called our supervisors. They weren't happy but once we explained what happened they understood. In the end, I was able to take the rest of the week off and meant to ask Riya to do the same but overheard him asking.

"You boys did the right thing, and this will give you time to decompress and get your affairs in order. But I do need to ask something of you," Jonovan said, and my heart fell.

Riya and my heads perked up as we glanced at each other and then at Jonovan. *Panic mode activated.* "It's nothing bad, well, not really. Artesia found out some information about Dominic, and it appears there have been other complaints about him and after seeing what I think he was behind at your apartment, I believe what she shared to be true. Let's get the bags inside and then we'll talk," Jonovan said. I was nervous to hear what he had to say and feared what this would do to Riya.

Silently we unloaded the car. Once inside, we took the tags off our clothes and Jonovan showed us where the washer was and how to use it. With our wash running, he asked us to have a seat at the dining table. Had any good conversations ever taken place around somebody's table? Not in my experience or in the movies I'd watched. It'd always been a breakup, or a death in the family, or a *hey, we lost the house and we're moving* type of shit.

"It's important to me that you both know your safety is number one where I'm concerned, and I will be here for you in whatever capacity you need me to be. If you chose for me to take over things in your day-to-day life I would, if there were only certain things you wanted me involved in, I'd respect your choices and stay in my lane. But the detectives have requested to interview both of you tomorrow. Artesia has offered up her office for us to meet in, though I wonder if you wouldn't be more comfortable meeting with them here?" Jonovan explained, doing his best to make us feel welcome though this wasn't our home.

I already knew my answer and I was fairly certain I knew Riya's as well. "I think we'd be more comfortable here."

"Yes," Riya easily agreed, though I knew tomorrow would be anything but easy for him.

"Thank you, boys, that's very brave of you and it's probably the only way this asshole will be stopped," Jonovan said. I didn't want to share too much, it wasn't my story to tell, but I also didn't want secrets kept between us. Our relationship was new, and the foundation must be built on trust. "When she spoke with the detectives, they shared that some of his victims wound up in the hospital with serious injuries." Riya's eyes widened, his mouth fell open and his eyes glossed over. "If you'd rather I not be in the room when you speak the detectives, I will respect your wishes."

Before Jonovan could finish that sentence, Riya spoke up. "I want you there. I need you and Stefan with me."

"As you wish, my sweet Kitten," Jonovan hugged Riya and I wrapped my arms around them. Riya was important to me, and I could clearly see we'd both become the same to Jonovan.

I loved the nicknames, how Jonovan called me sweet pup and Riya his sweet kitten, and Riya beamed each time he said it. His cheeks warmed and he got a gooey love-struck look on his face. Jonovan made us feel like we were wanted, and we belonged. I was comfortable and I knew Riya was, too, because I had never seen him come out of his shell this quickly or really at all before. I hoped today's events didn't set him back and forced Riya into hiding again. If so, hopefully Jonovan would know what to do to draw him back out. Our trust in Jonovan spoke volumes since neither of us trusted easily, or at all.

"Why don't you boys go for a swim? Titus loves the water," Jonovan said, and our ears perked up. On our days off during the week, while the others in our complex were at work, we'd hang out at the pool.

"Wait, you have a pool?" I asked. Last night the lights were off and the blinds were closed so we couldn't see outside, and this morning we'd left rather abruptly. Riya and I ran for the back door and straight out into the sun. "Is it okay to swim in our shorts? We didn't get any swim trunks," I asked. Riya wouldn't take his shirt off, so I'd wear one as well. I didn't want to call attention to him for being the only one wearing a shirt.

"Absolutely, go on out. I have a couple of calls to make, and I'll meet you guys outside afterward. I have steaks in the freezer I can set out. Would you guys like to barbeque for dinner, or would you prefer something else?" Jonovan hollered out the back door we'd left open.

"Yes, we're carnivores and steaks sound great," I replied, and mentally added up everything Jonovan had spent on us. Steaks were not cheap, and I couldn't picture him buying the bargain ones that were about to expire like we'd done many times.

We ran back inside, went into the room and stripped down to our boxers and t-shirts. It wasn't my story to tell as to why we kept our shirts on and although it was Riya's, he'd determine when he was comfortable enough to share it. Honestly, if we were meeting with the cops tomorrow, he'd have to tell the truth then. I had the feeling after that I'd be one of many standing in a long line waiting to take a turn at beating the shit out of Dominic.

As we passed by Jonovan's office he called out, "Towels are in the cupboard on the porch, soft drinks and water are in the mini-fridge under the outside bar. Have fun, boys, I'll be out shortly." It was so nice to have someone who cared.

"Thank you!" we yelled back. "Come on, Titus." As we went out the adult door, he darted out the dog door and met us on the other side. Slowly Riya and I slipped into the water step by step, as we tried to get our bodies acclimated to the water's temperature. Titus wasn't having any of that, he jumped right in and swam around in circles, happily barking.

"That dog is crazy," Riya said, and laughed the entire time as he watched our crazy new friend. I loved seeing Riya this happy and free. Let him enjoy tonight because tomorrow would be hard and I for one didn't look forward to it, and I only knew part of Riya's story. But there was no turning back now.

Not long after we'd fully submerged ourselves, Jonovan came out. Titus bounded out of the pool toward him and shook all the water off just as he reached Jonovan. "Gee, thanks, Titus," he complained, though it was half-assed. It was hard to be angry when the dog was cute as hell, plus he was jumping in anyway.

"Cannonball!" Jonovan hollered as he launched himself into the pool. Riya and I rode the wave back to shore, well, back to the stairs where we parked ourselves. Titus's mini cannonball followed his. Their antics had us cracking up. "Your laughter is infectious, my pets," Jonovan said as he swam over to us grinning from ear to ear. Titus decided to jump out and shake off all the water right behind us then he took off and zoomed around the yard like somebody had tickled him.

"Having a dog is fun," Riya said, his eyes clocking Titus's every move.

"Yeah, he's a real riot until his flatulence burns your nostrils," Jonovan complained.

"Ew, that does not sound fun," I cringed. "I can only imagine how bad that would smell. I wanted to be a Boxer initially as my breed when in pup form, but then I just decided not to choose any and just be me."

"That's a good choice, my little pup," Jonovan said as he leaned over to kiss me then Riya. "It makes you uniquely you.

"Do you have a favorite cat breed, Riya?" Jonovan asked him.

Raya shrugged. "Not really. I pretty much like all animals. Does Titus get along with cats?" Riya asked.

"That's a great question but one I don't know the answer to. I got him from a breeder when he was a puppy, he's AKC registered but I had him neutered as soon as he was of age to do so. He's never been around cats, though I'd like to think with his friendly disposition that he would be fine, but I've heard stories of Boxers playing too rough with cats and accidentally injuring them. He doesn't have a malicious bone in his body, and I believe he'd feel terrible if he did hurt one. Long story short, I've never tried. It's always just been the two of us," Jonovan shared and I detected a hint of loneliness to his words.

"Makes total sense," Riya said.

"What time do you guys want to eat?" Jonovan asked before he slid back under the water to wet his hair. God, he had that hot Daddy vibe going on. Every inch of him radiated sexiness from the salt and pepper hair to the matching beard, right down to the light smattering across his chest. Don't even get me started on the tattoos. His physique spoke to years of hard labor, and he was in excellent shape. I was a goofy teen all over again having my first crush on my high school science teacher. Thank the school gods nobody ever found out about that, or I really would have been tortured by my peers.

I leaned back and soaked up the sun's rays as it heated my skin and watched our hot Daddy swim. It was nice to be outdoors, not having to worry about when we needed to bail before the pool filled with screaming kids. This was perfect, the three of us and Titus. Jonovan's outdoor space was just as inviting as the inside. The porch ran the length of the house and completely shaded the BBQ area which was built into an L-shaped bar with concrete countertops. Beneath it there was a wine and mini-fridge.

The pool deck extended well past the perimeter of the pool and there were two lounge chairs off to the side. It was comfortable without being over the top, just like the interior. The entire place was built to be one of Zen, a place to relax and not to be a showcase home in some architectural magazine.

“Who decorated your house?” I blurted out the random question and caught him off guard.

“I did,” Jonovan replied, “do you like it?”

“I really do. It's not one of those houses where you're afraid to touch something or move it an inch to the right and have the homeowner scream at you. It’s comfortable, I really like it,” I admitted, though I didn’t know why. It wasn’t like my opinion mattered.

“Me, too,” Riya chimed in. “Your backyard is great.”

“I'm glad you two approve,” Jonovan winked as he hopped out of the pool and grabbed his towel. “Let me get the barbeque warmed up.”

“What can we do to help?” I asked as I grabbed two towels and handed one to Riya.

“Well, that depends. Do you want to eat inside or out?” Jonovan asked.

“Outside!” Riya and I cheered.

“Outside it is then. While I cook the steaks, why don't you scrounge around inside for side dishes. I think there is some leftover salad in the fridge, possibly some chips or beans in the pantry. Pick whatever you like and bring it out. Sound good to you?"

"Sure does," I replied just as my stomach grumbled.

Chapter Nine

Riya

I couldn't sleep at all. I'd moved around so much both Jonovan and Stefan rolled over away from me during the night. The one good thing about that was it allowed me to slip out of bed unnoticed. Down the hall I went with Titus alongside me. "Let's see what's on TV," I said to him as we curled up on the couch. Stefan was used to my nights of challenged sleep and turning on random shows to watch until my brain settled down, but I didn't want to bother Jonovan. He'd been so nice to us that the last thing I wanted to do was upset him. This was only our second night sleeping here and I was thankful I'd not had any nightmares. Yet. Tomorrow, well, there was no way it wasn't going to suck but I hoped it didn't cause one.

An old black and white comedy show was on. This woman and her co-worker worked on a conveyor belt sorting chocolate candy. Somehow, it sped up and she couldn't keep up with it and so she started eating some and shoving other chocolates down her work top. I didn't quite understand how it got so out of control, but it was funny to see where she'd try and stuff the pieces next. One episode led to another and before I knew it, I was out but somehow I woke up in Jonovan's bed in the morning.

"Good morning," I mumbled, wiping the sleep from my eyes as I entered the kitchen.

"Good morning, Kitten," Jonovan greeted me with a kiss.

"Where's Stefan?" I grabbed a mug from the cupboard and poured a cup of coffee, and deeply inhaled my favorite morning scent.

"Out back with Titus," Jonovan replied as he flipped the pancakes. "Hungry?"

"Meh." Wasn't much of a reply but with my stomach in knots I wasn't sure eating was the best thing for it.

"Riya, you need something on your stomach. Sweetheart," Jonovan said as he wrapped an arm around my waist and pulled me to him. "I know you're nervous, but Stefan and I will be right there beside you."

He had zero idea what level my nerves were at and I was afraid he'd see me as not worthy of him after today killed me. Jonovan had been nothing but wonderful to us, but would he be able to deal with...I shuddered. The fear was real, and the reality of my truth may very well end the dreamland Stefan and I currently enjoyed. Maybe they'd be better off without me, happier as a normal couple instead of a throple. It took all I had not to burst into tears, I'd wasted far too much time crying lately. I'd always been an emotional wreck and wouldn't be surprised if I was once again kicked to the curb after all this was over.

"Whatever you're thinking, Riya," Stefan's voice came from behind me. "Erase it."

"Kitten?" Jonovan asked as he pulled back. "What's going on?"

I couldn't speak my worst fears alive. "Let me guess," Stefan began. "You're thinking after today when the truth comes out, we won't want you around. You're not good enough for us and you'll get rejected. Am I right?"

I said nothing.

"Riya, if you're that nervous just show him," Stefan said, and I froze.

"Stefan, please don't force him to do something he's not comfortable with," Jonovan said.

"It's going to come out later and he needs to see that you won't reject him because of it. Riya, none of this is your fault. I know you think it is, but you're wrong. We won't reject you," Stefan replied. "Ever."

"Riya, there is nothing you could show me that would make me push you away. Don't you get it? I'm in too deep with you and Stefan, you're my boys," Jonovan did his best to reassure me but under this shirt I was ugly, and I didn't want him to see it. If he rejected me at my most vulnerable it would crush me to a point I'd never recover from. "Come on, boys. Let's eat." I appreciated Jonovan not pushing the issue. Soon enough, he'd see the hideous freak beneath the clothes.

Not a word was said as we ate and then cleaned the kitchen. Stefan was the first to shower while I played with Titus, then it was my turn. Mentally, I did my best to psych myself up. "It'll be all right," I spoke into the fogged-up bathroom mirror. "If not, you rebuild again. Maybe this time you'll come out of it even stronger." Even my brain couldn't stick with the power of positivity. For every positive, it kicked out a negative. A tightwire balancing act that always left me empty.

I was sitting on the bed when Stefan opened the bedroom door and came inside. "Are you okay?" he asked.

"No. We can't stay here, living a dream that isn't ours. We need to get back to reality. Jonovan's only being nice because he feels bad for us. He probably just wants his space back and would feel guilty kicking us out," I said, though I knew the words weren't true. But if we got angry enough it would help get past the pain.

"How do you know?" Stefan whispered. His face reflected the sorrow he felt, which was all my fault. How could I do this, say these terrible things to someone I loved and about someone I was falling for? What the fuck was wrong with me?

"Well," Jonovan said as he stepped inside the room and startled Stefan and me. "You could start by asking me instead of assuming you know what I want." My face flushed. Busted.

"Sorry," I muttered.

Jonovan came over and sat between us. "Riya, there is absolutely nothing that can be said today that would make me feel less about you. About either of you." He took our hands in his. "None of this is your fault and you're here because I want you here. Not only to help you, but to help me. It's selfish on my part but I want you with me and I dread the day you might..." He stared down at our combined hands in his lap. My gut clenched and I wanted to punch myself for being such a fucking asshole. "But if you want to leave, I'll understand."

Before anymore hurtful things could be said, the doorbell rang. Stefan and I stayed in the room while Jonovan answered the door and returned a few moments later. "When you boys are ready, they're here." Jonovan turned and left the room. His sadness was also on my hands. I'd now managed to hurt both the men I cared about, and I couldn't hate myself more than I did right then.

"Let's go," Stefan said as he followed Jonovan out.

"Deep breath, Riya. Nothing can hurt more than the shit you just pulled," I cursed myself aloud. I tried to calm my nerves then dove into the fiery pit to share the story of the greatest mistake of my life. One that cost me my soul and nearly ended my life.

"Stefan, Riya, this is Detective Ambrose and his partner, Detective Morton," Jonovan said as we came into the living room, Artesia stood beside him. Everyone took a seat, Jonovan, Stefan, and I on the couch. Even though neither of them were happy with me, hell, I wasn't happy with me, I was still thankful they were near.

"Gentlemen," Detective Ambrose began, "Do you mind if we record this?" He pulled a pocket-sized device from his pocket and held it up for us to see.

"That's fine," Stefan replied, I'm sure he thought it might move this along and get it over with quicker.

"Riya?" Detective Ambrose asked.

"It's okay," Riya answered, nervously twisting his hands in his lap.

"Thank you," Detective Ambrose replied. "Let's start with how you first met Dominic Slater."

"It was on Craigslist," Stefan said. "We wanted to learn more about pet play but couldn't afford the expensive clubs or gear. He claimed to be a Dom and seasoned handler and even said he had some old gear we could have. It started off well, he said all the right things and got us into the club. We watched a few scenes then he insisted on driving us home. The second time we got together was much the same, but it was the third time that took a bad turn."

"How so?" Detective Morton asked and Stefan glanced at me.

"Riya and I split up that night. I wanted to explore more than the pet play and you know, see what else was out there. Dominic said he'd train with Riya. It started getting late and people were leaving so I went in search of Riya. All the doors were open but one," Stefan paused. My heart rate accelerated at an alarming rate as I recalled that night and I thought for sure I was on the verge of a heart attack. "Riya was," Jonovan reached over, once again taking our hands in his. "Riya was still tied up, naked, and covered in blood." Jonovan gasped and Artesia hung her head while the detectives continued taking notes.

"Riya?" Detective Ambrose asked. "I know this is difficult, but it's important you tell us what took place."

Once, twice, I swallowed hard and my throat went dry. "We, um, we went inside the room. It wasn't a pet playroom, it was a dungeon and he locked the door behind us." I recalled his every word, the terror I felt then filled me again. "'I finally got you alone. Come, Riya, let me show you what it means to be my sub.' I told him this wasn't the right room and went for the door, that's when things took a bad turn." Now was not the time for an anxiety attack but I teetered on the edge of one. While I took a few moments to compose myself, Jonovan left and returned with water bottles for everyone. I was thankful, for him and the drink.

"I did my best to fight him off, but that only seemed to excite him more. He grabbed me by the throat and said if I moved again, he'd beat my ass. I stood there as he took off all my clothes and chained me to the big cross on the wall. He picked up a couple of whips and started hitting me with them. I was in and out of consciousness and repeatedly told him no and called out red, but he wouldn't listen. That's when he," I paused, *you can do this, Riya, you've come this far so there's no turning back now.* "That's when he raped me."

"Riya," Stefan began to cry beside me.

"I take it Stefan didn't know about that?" Officer Morton asked.

"No, he assumed all the blood came from the gashes," I replied. Fuck, I wanted to run away and hide and never see any of their faces again. This fucking sucked, reliving it a second time was nearly as bad as the first.

"After he was done, he laughed and said he was through with me and left. I don't know how long I was there before Stefan found me," I finished.

"Riya, I hate to ask this but are there any visible scars that remain? We need to photograph them as evidence," Officer Morton asked. This was the part I dreaded most, though I knew it was inevitable. What would Jonovan think of me after this?

I glanced at Stefan for guidance, "You can do this, Riya. We need to get him off the streets before he hurts someone else, or worse, kills them."

I reached for the hem of my shirt and closed my eyes as I removed it and spun around so my back faced the detective. I couldn't bear to look into their eyes for fear of what I might see. Would they reflect disgust, or pity? Neither were reactions I was prepared to deal with. Either one would break me into pieces that wouldn't mend.

"Thank you, Riya," Officer Ambrose said a few moments later. "You can put your shirt back on."

"Dominic is a predator who preys on young novices via Craigslist and other sites that aren't monitored as strictly as they should be. He's been banned from every local club and many of us have networked beyond our own states to ensure the community is aware," Artesia spoke for the first time. "I'm sorry this happened to you, Riya, and I will do everything in my power to right this wrong."

The detectives stayed about fifteen minutes longer, and asked questions such as do you know anyone else who he's interacted with? No, we didn't. Do you know where he lives or works? No, we don't. I gave him the phone number we had for him, I had him blocked on my phone but in order to do that I couldn't delete the contact itself. I just did my best to ignore that horrible name anytime I scrolled through my contacts.

Stefan and I curled up on the couch and silently reflected while Jonovan walked them out. Titus sensed something was wrong and jumped up beside us. After everyone was gone, Jonovan came over and sat on the coffee table adjacent to us and all I could think was, here it comes...

Chapter Ten

Jonovan

I wanted to bash his fucking skull in. I was ready to hunt that worthless piece of shit down and fucking end him. Never had I seen red as I did right then. Never had I wanted to take a human life as much as I did right at this very moment and that scared the hell out of me. Who would take care of these sweet boys who'd been through so much in their short lives if I were gone?

"Boys," my voice cracked, the emotions overwhelmed me. "Dear God."

"Please, don't pity me," Riya snarled.

"Pity? No. Pity isn't what I feel. Anger, hate, and a few other emotions that would ensure a quick ride to the gates of hell currently flow through me." Riya's eyes widened at my admission. Stefan's face reflected some of what I felt. He too was angry, and he'd been privy to part of this already, but obviously not to the biggest part.

No means no.

End. Of. Fucking. Story.

You did not take what was not offered.

Riya bowed his head and stared down. Zero self-esteem thanks to all the fuckers that had passed through his life. Riya had no idea how utterly beautiful he was, so *purrfect*. "My sweet Kitten, none of this was your fault and don't you think for a second that it was. Riya," I reached over and tucked a strand of hair behind his ear, and he leaned into my palm. "You are beautiful, inside and out. Both of you are." I turned my eyes to Stefan so he could see the honesty of my words reflected in them. "You boys have become my world, and nothing could make me feel otherwise. If you chose to leave today, I'd honor your request, but I'd be completely heartbroken."

"You think I'm beautiful?" Riya whispered.

"Yes, my beautiful Kitten, I do."

"Even with the scars?"

"The scars hold no weight in how I feel about you. They speak to your strength and the battles you've fought and won. You are a survivor, Riya. I hate what you've had to endure, the pain you've had to live with, but it made you the man that you are today. One of the two men that hold the key to my heart," I admitted. I'd laid it all out there and maybe that would help ease their worried minds. No more talks of me kicking them to the curb. No question of how I felt about them.

"Riya, why didn't you tell me?" Stefan asked, tears streaming down his face. "I'm so fucking sorry."

"Oh, Stefan," Riya hugged him, "this isn't your fault. You have nothing to be sorry for."

"I should've stayed with you that night. It was selfish of me to go off on my own. I'll never leave you again, I swear," Stefan promised, though that wouldn't be fair to Riya. There would be things that Riya would need to do and experience on his own and as much as I wanted to protect Riya, and Stefan for that matter, I couldn't possibly be by their sides twenty-four hours a day.

"Boys, I need to hold you. Can you humor an old man?" A little self-deprecating humor might lighten the moment. They scooted apart enough for me to slide between them and wrap my arms around them. One boy on each side felt like...*home.* We had a long road ahead of us and I would have to earn their trust, which I would do. *All good things come to those who wait*, my momma used to say, and these boys were more than worth the wait.

"How about a nice, relaxing day at home, maybe binge watch mindless TV?" I suggested.

"That sounds perfect to me," Riya replied. Stefan would take some time to work past the guilt, as would I even though I wasn't there. When you cared for someone, you cared with your whole heart, and it was clear Stefan and I were in the same boat when it came to Riya. How different my boys were. Unique and perfect.

My boys.

I'd said it a couple of times already but that was when it really sank in. Stefan, the proud, strong one with a soft inside. Riya, the gentle, shy one who wore his heart on his sleeve. Two completely different men yet two that I loved and would protect with my life. I loved them in my space, our space, and hoped like hell they'd never leave.

When you know you just...know.

I squeezed my boys a little tighter, their heads nested on my chest and their intertwined fingers atop my stomach. This was the life, what I'd been missing. Through tragedy came bonding, strength, and even love. While they might not feel as strongly about me as I did them while they still guarded their hearts, I'd expect nothing less after what they'd been through. But I knew with time, they'd feel the same, though I'd have to pull back my own reins so I didn't overwhelm them.

Artesia called while I made lunch and asked if we'd represent her float at the annual Phoenix Pride Parade. I was honored to be asked but told her I'd get back with her after

I spoke to the boys. When we sat down to eat, I broached the subject.

"Have you been to the Phoenix Pride Parade?" I asked them.

"No," Stefan replied.

"Me neither," Riya added.

"Artesia asked if we'd represent the Blue Underground and ride on their float or walk alongside it. What do you think?" I asked.

"Will there be others there?" Stefan asked.

"Yes, and all will be in their gear as well or donning their leathers. Doms, subs, pets, littles, and their Daddies—you name it," I replied, my eagerness to attend shone through. The idea of being there with Pup and Kitty filled me with a warmth I couldn't explain.

"I think it would be fun. What do you think, Riya?" Stefan asked.

Riya shrugged. "It's gonna be a lot of people and you know I don't people well," Riya admitted, and my heart fell. My poor Kitty, top item on my list was to build his self-esteem.

"For the most part, we will be with the floats and the crowds would be off to the side. Plus, Stefan and I won't leave you. If it becomes too overwhelming all you have to do is tell us you've had enough and we are out of there," I said.

"Promise?" Riya asked, those big blue eyes searched mine for the truth.

"Promise. Riya, no means no in all aspects of your life. I will always, always, respect that with zero hard feelings. Ever," I assured him.

He stared at me for a few seconds longer then bobbed his head. "Yeah, okay."

Over the next few weeks, the boys returned to work, and I changed my schedule to work more from home. I promoted my assistant to manager and was training her to take over more of my duties. She knew this industry inside and out having been in it for twenty plus years in one role or another. Hell, she'd even been on the labor side of it as a tech for several years and took no shit from anyone. The men respected her as did I and I knew she was the perfect fit. It was time for me to live my life for me and not continue to bury myself in work. My team was fully capable of running the show without me there on a daily basis.

I'd taken the liberty of ordering the boys new gear. Pup was a fan of all things blue, and Kitty's go to color was purple, but they'd only been able to afford used gear until now. Everything arrived just in time for tomorrow's parade. I had planned an elaborate private dinner at home during which I'd present them with their gifts. Was it too much? My boys weren't the type to demand or even expect gifts and at times seemed a bit uncomfortable with receiving them. Great, now I worried I'd gone overboard.

The boys moving in was a seamless transition even though the circumstances that surrounded the impromptu decision to do so was anything but. They took direction well and preferred to have me provide them with tasks to complete, chores if you will. Less asking and more praise for jobs well done. They flourished under my nurturing hand, and I was putty in theirs.

By the time we finished lunch, I was a jittery ball of excitement and could barely contain myself. "Why don't you two go in the living room and I'll be there in a minute," I said as I darted from the room to my office where the gifts were hidden. Stefan and Riya exchanged quizzical glances before they followed the request. Moments later, I stood before them with two bags and boxes in hand. "I hope you don't mind, but I took the liberty of picking out a few things for you. I hope it's not too much." Would they like them? Did I overshoot? As they reached into the bags, the second guesses continued to beat me down.

One by one they pulled the gifts out, their eyes alight and when they finally smiled, I breathed a sigh of relief.

"Oh, Daddy," Riya surprised me by saying the word I'd longed to hear for the first time. "So. Much. Pretty. Purple. Thank you." He dove into my lap and peppered my face with kisses.

"This is wonderful, Daddy. Everything is in my favorite color," Stefan said, and then my lap was filled with two wonderful boys.

"I know, Pup. But there's more." The next gifts would be a big step for us. One I was ready for, but were they? I handed them each a box, their eyes widened once they saw what was inside. "I know they're not the traditional colors for collar ceremonies and I skipped like three steps, but we aren't traditional, really. Boys, I would be honored if you'd wear my collars and be my lifelong partners."

"Daddy," Stefan barely choked the words out. The moment they uttered the word my heart took off in flight and soared around us, sealing the bond. "I love it. Please put it on me."

"Me, too! Me, too!" Riya excitedly chanted. Often times I wondered if he wouldn't enjoy being a pup as well on occasion.

Tears filled my eyes. This was such an honor and the perfect moment to collar them. First, I fitted Stefan's royal blue and black leather collar with a shiny silver paw-shaped tag that read '*Pup, I belong to Daddy Jonovan*' around his slender neck. Then turned to Riya and secured his eggplant and black leather collar with matching tag that read '*Kitty, I belong to Daddy Jonovan*' around his dainty neck. Their smiles lit up my world and filled me with a sense of pride, our own pride aside from the community we were a part of.

"You boys don't need to wear these all the time if you don't want to, but it would mean the world to me if you'd wear them for the parade and when we played," I said, and felt like a silly young boy asking his date, or dates in this case, to the prom. Maybe I should've slipped a note into their lockers?

"These shirts are so silly, I love them, Daddy," Riya said, as he read the lettering of the custom-made tees aloud. "I'm with Daddy Jonovan. Look at the arrow, Stefan, it's made of paw prints."

"Mine says the same. Turn yours over, Riya," on the back I'd printed the word *Pup* on Stefan's and *Kitty* on Riya's. I had one as well that said *I belong to Pup and Kitty* with *Daddy Jonovan* on the back. As of late, Stefan had claimed my right side and Riya the left so each of their arrows pointed toward me and I'd be between them tomorrow.

I got Stefan a new hood that matched his collar in the same royal blue and black. Riya got a new pink kitty nose on a purple and black mask with whiskers included. Both received two tails, one a surface unit with a belt strap and the other a butt plug version. Each a pair of black booty shorts and leashes that matched their masks.

"My turn, Daddy," Riya said, holding his collar up.

"You boys have made me a very happy Daddy and I love you both so much." While I'd mentioned love several times, this was the first time I'd actually said the words aloud in their entirety.

"I love you, too, Daddy," Stefan said and rubbed noses with me before he pressed his lips to mine.

Riya curled up on my lap and nudged Stefan a side. "Oh, Daddy," he purred, "I love you, too," and then he too kissed me. Tears freely flowed amongst the three of us though for the first time since we met, they were tears of joy.

Chapter Eleven

Stefan

We'd been living with Jonovan, *Daddy*, for several weeks now and I'd not initiated anything sexual because I didn't want Riya to feel uncomfortable. Riya and I hadn't done anything anal since that night at the club and I felt like such an idiot for not putting two and two together. I just wrote it off as neither of us liked to top and accepted our future would only include blowjobs and frotting and I was perfectly okay with that. But as of late, I'd been thinking about it. Sex that is. A lot. And after Daddy collared us today, it was time. At least for me it was. I wanted Daddy to mark me as his and claim me in all ways possible. I was his. If Riya wanted to wait, that was completely up to him. I'd never push him into doing anything he didn't want to, and I knew Daddy wouldn't either.

"Why are you fidgeting, Stefan?" Daddy asked me during dinner. Nervously, I tugged at my collar. "If the collar is bothering you, you don't have to wear it."

"It's not that," I paused. *Come on, Stefan, you've never been the king of subtle so blurt it out.* "I want to have sex. Anal sex. With you."

Riya choked and Daddy ran to his side and patted him on the back. When Riya reached for his drink, Daddy visibly relaxed. "Oh, um, okay?" Daddy half questioned. "Just so I'm clear, to whom exactly are you making this offer?"

"To you. Tonight. Please." Wow, I was fucking this up big time. And to top it off I was coming off like an immature virgin. Who in their right mind would want to tap that? I shook my head and groaned. "Ugh, so sorry. I just," I paused. "I'm ready. I want that with you. I want to be yours in all ways."

"Thank you, Stefan. I'm honored," Daddy kissed the top of my head as he passed by and sat back down.

"Do you have condoms and lube?" I blurted out, my brain-mouth filter was completely absent today. Riya again choked. That boy needed to learn how to chew his food. "Sorry." I was excited, in more ways than one, and couldn't seem to contain it.

This time, Daddy laughed. "Yes, my eager Pup, I have condoms and lube, though I would like for the three of us to get tested soon if that's all right with both of you?"

"Yes, please," I immediately replied. Riya continued shifting what remained of his food around on his plate. "Sorry, Riya." Today I should just put out a blanket apology to the world so I wouldn't have to repeat the word again.

"Riya, my sweet Kitten," Daddy reached across the table and placed his hand over Riya's. "Please do not feel obligated to get tested or do anything you're not comfortable with. I love you no matter what and sex isn't a deal breaker for me."

"Thank you, Daddy," he whispered, and I had to hug him.

"Do you have a problem with Stefan and I engaging in anything sexual?" Daddy asked him. "We can refrain or go into another room if you'd prefer."

"No, Daddy. I don't want you to do that, this is your house," Riya replied.

"Our house," Daddy corrected him.

"Maybe I could, umm," Riya nervously shifted in his seat. "Maybe I could watch? Or touch? Just not, you know."

"Whatever you want, sweet boy," Daddy replied. Our Daddy was the best, so gentle and caring, and he loved Riya and I fiercely.

After dinner we went for a swim. Each time Daddy passed by us while doing laps he'd stop and give us a kiss. It was so freaking cute. My dick, though, had me on the verge of tears. It was painfully hard and I swear if anyone touched me right now, I'd launch into orbit. It had been so long since I'd come. Between our apartment getting broken into and dealing with the police, then getting acclimated to our new lives, I hadn't really thought about it and yet today I couldn't get it off my mind.

"All right," Daddy said as he got out of the pool. "I think our Pup is about to explode, Kitty. Time to get out."

He couldn't be more right.

"Okay, my squirrelly pets, go shower and I'll meet you in the bedroom." Daddy was all smiles, at least my over anxiousness hadn't upset him. If anything, it appeared he enjoyed it. Riya and I showered together as we'd been doing since we moved in. Daddy had a massive shower that the three of us could easily fit in, though he'd not asked to join us. Riya slid into a pair of boxers, and I hopped in bed as naked as the day I was born, half-hard cock swinging between my legs as I bounced around.

When Daddy walked in and saw me, he laughed. "Trying to give Titus a run for his money, Pup?" Daddy asked.

I never quite grasped that saying, I mean, a dog didn't have money. Right?

"Just. So. Excited," I said the words with each hop. "And horny." My dick waved proudly as if saying, *look at me, look at me!*

"So, I can see. Give me a few minutes and I'll join you." Daddy shut the bathroom door and I heard the shower turn on.

"You okay, Riya?" I asked.

"Yeah," he murmured, but that wasn't good enough.

I flipped around and straddled him, "Do you want us to not do this?" I asked, mentally chanting, *please say no, please say no.*

"No, it's just, umm," he flexed up and was he...*hard?* Was it possible the thought of Daddy fucking me aroused him?

I leaned in and kissed him. One kiss led to another, soon tongues were involved, and that's how Daddy found us when he came out of the shower. Skin glistening with water droplets, towel around his waist. "Now that is a sight I wouldn't mind seeing more of," he said as he dropped the towel and I whimpered. "See something you like, Pup?" Daddy said with a wink. I'd not seen him fully naked yet. He'd been very careful how he presented himself around us. Always the gentleman and careful of our comfort and feelings.

"Yes, Daddy. Very much." Would licking my lips be too much?

He lay on his side, half-hard cock resting against his thigh. I wanted to... "Whoa, Pup," Daddy moaned as I took him to the back of my throat. "That feels. That feels..." he trailed off as I moved to the tip and sucked a bit harder. "So good."

I could feel Riya's eyes on us. What was he thinking? How did he feel? A quick head to toe scan answered that. He and Daddy held hands while Riya's other slowly stroked his own cock. Maybe this wasn't such a bad idea after all.

"Sweet Pup," Daddy called out as he ran his fingers through my hair. "You don't want to make Daddy come too soon. Roll over." I slid off with a pop and landed on my back so fast Riya bounced. "My eager boy." Daddy slid a hand down my torso and firmly gripped my cock.

"Daddy," I moaned. I loved the feel of his hand on my skin. The gentle strokes and heated looks. Dear gods, this man was the whole package.

"Riya, would you like to fuck Daddy's mouth?" he asked. I swear my heart stopped as we waited for Riya to reply.

"Um, okay." This was probably the best way to reacclimate Riya into the world of intimacy as it gave him complete control. He slid out of his boxers and knee-walked across the bed toward Daddy.

"That's Daddy's good boy," Daddy opened wide, and Riya tentatively slid inside. Daddy continued to jerk me as Riya slowly slid in and out of Daddy's mouth.

"Fuck, you guys are killing me," I complained and counted backwards from fifty to keep from coming. Riya shivered and pulled out at the same time.

"Turn over, Pup. Let Daddy get you ready." It had been a while for me so I was thankful Daddy mentioned prep. "Riya, why don't you slide beneath Stefan so you two can play while Daddy teases our Pup?"

Daddy grabbed a condom and lube from the bedside table while Riya scooted under me. Our lips were like magnets as they once again met. Riya and I never had a problem turning each other on and kissing was one of our favorite things. I'd come many times from that alone when we messed around before.

"Jesus, you two are so beautiful together," Daddy said as he pushed a finger inside me. The burn of the initial penetration gave me pause but soon enough, I pressed back, fucking myself against the digit and put on a show for Daddy. When he was three fingers deep, I was more than ready and nearly over the edge.

"Now, Daddy, please," I shamelessly begged. The condom wrapper was torn open and tossed aside and soon the head of his cock pressed against the tight ring of muscle and slowly pushed inside. I stilled, though only for a moment. That initial discomfort was fleeting, a precursor to the pleasure I knew would come. Once Daddy was fully seated inside me, he gave me time to adjust before he pulled out and slammed back in. I opened my eyes to find Riya staring up at me. "Are you okay?" I asked him.

He bit his bottom lip and replied, "Yes. This is so much hotter than I imagined." Well, at least I knew that he had thought about sex which was a step in the right direction.

"Stroke Riya, Stefan," Daddy directed just as he hit the spot and I howled.

"Fuck, right there. Yes, Daddy," I moaned and took Riya and my cocks in hand and stroked them to the beat of Daddy's thrusts.

"Boys, Daddy won't last much longer," Daddy panted, and I was in much the same state. I stroked harder, faster. Riya and I were covered in sweat, barely holding back.

"Stefan," my name ghosted across Riya's lips as he came. That single word sent me over the edge.

"Fuck, oh fuck," I groaned as my orgasm hit.

"Oh god," Daddy growled as he pulsed inside me. Filling me as deep as he could go and claiming me in the ultimate way.

Heavy breaths filled the room, the smell of sweat and sex permeated the air. I hadn't realized how badly I'd needed that release until this very moment. I had an inkling but once the door opened, it hit like a fucking hurricane. Daddy fell to the side and took me with him.

"I love you, boys," Daddy panted.

"Love you, Daddy," we murmured, already half asleep. Sometime later I felt Daddy wipe us clean and Riya and I moved to our usual sleeping spots with Riya between Daddy and me, and then we passed out.

"No! Stop! Please stop!" Riya cried out, and kicked his legs while and he twisted them up in the sheets. "Please stop!"

"What's happening?" Daddy asked me.

"He's having a nightmare about Dominic." The guilt I felt deepened and hit me like a punch to the gut.

"What do we do?" Daddy worriedly asked.

"Speak softly, let him know he's okay," I said and turned to Riya. "Riya, baby, it's me, Stefan. You're okay."

"Riya, sweetheart, it's Daddy. Can you please wake up, Kitten?" Daddy whispered.

Riya bolted upright so fast he nearly conked our skulls. First, he turned to me, then to Daddy, and burst into tears before he curled up against Daddy's chest. I hugged him from behind, and Daddy wound his arms around him while we continued to whisper sweet things to him.

"Riya, we love you. No one will ever hurt you again," Daddy told him. "Ssh, baby boy," Daddy rocked him back and forth. "You're safe. It's okay."

"Riya, baby, the bad man is gone," I said. He hadn't had a nightmare since we moved in. Did Daddy and I having sex trigger this episode? I sure as fuck hoped not. Maybe Daddy and I needed to talk to him about seeing a therapist or someone who could help him. After hearing Riya's story, I couldn't imagine how scared and helpless he felt that night. Eventually, Riya's sobs quieted, and his breaths evened out as he fell back to sleep.

I hoped that fucking bastard got what was coming to him in a fucking prison cell by a man who barely fit through the door.

Far too soon, the alarm clock on Daddy's phone sounded. I didn't think Daddy, nor I fell into a deep sleep.

Chapter Twelve

Riya

"Welcome one and all to the annual Phoenix Pride Parade!" The grand marshal's announcement from atop his elaborate float was met with the loudest cheers and whistles I'd ever heard. It was hard not to be excited when you were surrounded by smiling faces and bright, colorful rainbow decorations. I'd never seen anything like it.

"I'm honored to be here today surrounded by community members and allies alike." While he continued his speech, Daddy helped us get into our gear. We'd walk in human form today, but we still dressed out for it. I for one was glad the parade happened in November and not June or we'd likely suffer heat stroke from the brutal summer heat.

One by one the floats entered the designated path for today's parade route, each one was designed to represent the company who'd sponsored it. Ours was beautiful, decked out in various shades of blue and black with a logoed banner that matched the signage at the Blue Underground. Artesia, Mistress Artesia I'd recently learned, gave us each a handful of Mardi Gras beads to hand out to the bystanders as we passed them by. Stefan and I proudly wore our collars from Daddy, we rarely took them off except to shower and sleep. At first my boss wasn't happy about it but, in the end, she shook it off and let it go. I didn't care one way or another how she felt, I was proud to wear Daddy's collar and knew if I quit or got fired, he wouldn't fuss. To Daddy all that mattered was that Riya and I were happy.

I never imagined in a million years I could ever be this happy.

When New Order's song "Blue Monday" began to play, that was our queue to hit the trail. We had the option of riding on the float with the dancers or walking around it. We opted to walk around it otherwise the cute shirts Daddy got us wouldn't work as well and we wanted to show them and our Daddy off. This way, Daddy was in the middle with our paw arrows proudly pointing at him.

Our Daddy was the best.

One of many wishes were fulfilled by this wonderful man between us. Not only having a Daddy but a Daddy who wanted us, too. From the moment I first called Jonovan Daddy, everything felt right in ways I couldn't explain.

People smiled and waved from the sidelines, families from all walks of life coming together in celebration. Mothers who wore shirts that offered free hugs, and I had to admit I took several of them up on it. Hugs were the best. I slid shiny beaded necklaces over the children's heads, they'd smile and say thank you. The whole scene was too dang cute. Babies in strollers decked out in rainbow wear, men who wore next to nothing which was a little scary and oddly hot at the same time. It was adorable when I'd walk up to them, and they'd call out *Kitty* and point at my mask. I did a little dance that made them laugh and then I'd skip back toward Daddy and Pup. Pup was thoroughly enjoying himself, too, and Daddy was all smiles as he watched his boys.

I couldn't help but move to the music. It was a happy time, a day of celebration, or at least it was in Phoenix and the best part was I got to share it with Daddy and Stefan. Daddy said we could stay for the after parties and check out some of the booths if we wanted. I was interested to see what the vendors had for sale but as far as parties went that really wasn't mine or Stefan's scene. We were happy homebodies, especially now in our cocoon of three, plus Titus of course, where we were free to be ourselves.

Daddy had everything we needed at home. Why waste money going out to a club when neither of us drank? And if we wanted to dance and be silly, we could just turn on the music at home and go to town. But today was a special day and to personally be invited by Mistress Artesia was a big deal. And though she graciously added Stefan and I to Daddy's membership, we'd only been back once for playtime. We had too much fun at home with the obstacle course that Daddy set up for us. Stefan and I got to roll around on the floor dressed up in our gear. Titus was curious, and he'd come over and try to steal our toys, but we always got them back. If we didn't then Daddy would and of course he would insist they be washed before he let us play with them again.

When the end of the parade route neared, I handed out the last of my beads. As I turned to walk back toward Daddy, out the corner of my eye, I saw a man push his way through the crowd. The sun reflected off something shiny he had in his hand, and it took me a moment to realize...

Dominic.

I froze. Before my brain engaged and alerted me to run, he lunged at me. I screamed as a hand wrapped around my waist and pulled me out of the way at the same time two men tackled Dominic to the ground. I recognized one of them as Detective Ambrose. I was in shock, time stood still but the parade moved on around me in muted tones.

Daddy, Stefan, and I were ushered off to the side. I shook uncontrollably as my body worked through the choices of do I vomit or pass out? Daddy must've sensed the internal struggle because his and Stefan's arms tightened around me. They weren't letting anyone near me and they wouldn't let me fall either. I knew it was Daddy who pulled me out of the way when Dominic lunged at me without having to ask. His arm hadn't left me since that very moment.

Once Dominic was hauled away and out of sight, Detective Morris approached us. "Gentlemen, I know you have a lot of questions and I'm willing to answer them, but it's imperative we get Dominic down to the station and book him. There's been a lot of new developments since we last met but this is not the appropriate setting to fill you in. We'll need to get your statements, though, but there isn't time for that now. I'll be in touch tomorrow and have you come down to the station to fill out the necessary paperwork.

"Yes, of course. Thank you, Detective," Daddy said. Detective Morris nodded and disappeared into the crowd. I was thankful very few heads turned our way and minded their own business. At least now I knew once and for all that Dominic would be behind bars and hopefully that would put an end to the nightmares. Daddy was so scared after last night and I didn't like seeing him that way. When I woke up this morning curled up in his arms and recalled what happened I was beyond embarrassed, but Daddy told me it wasn't my fault and I had nothing to worry about. He promised that he and Stefan would always be there for me. There wasn't a doubt in my mind that was true.

We walked back to the building where we'd left our stuff and changed into our regular clothes. By then, the three of us were more than ready to go home. As we were leaving, Artesia approached us.

"What was all the commotion about?" she asked.

"Dominic," Daddy said. "He was here. He tried to," his voice broke off. "He had a knife." If Daddy cried, I'd lose my shit.

"Oh my god," Artesia said. "Honey, are you okay?" she asked me, her eyes scanning my body for any sign of injuries.

"Yes, Daddy saved me," I replied.

"My God, Jonovan. I can't imagine," she was nearly as shaken up as we were.

Daddy squeezed me tight and pulled Stefan against his other side. It would be a long time before he let either one of us out of his sight, and I was more than fine with that.

"Thank you for inviting us here today, Artesia, but I'm going to take my boys home and never let them go," Daddy told her.

"I completely understand that," Artesia agreed and hugged us before we left. The garage where our truck was parked wasn't far yet it was too far. All I wanted was to get inside, lock the doors and go home. Even though I knew Dominic had been apprehended I was still jumpy, and every little noise had me squeezing Daddy's hand tighter. I clutched his arm like a life preserver and breathed a sigh of relief once we were on the road. After we got home and were safely locked inside, I felt like I could breathe again. The three of us, and Titus of course, curled up on the couch and stayed that way for the rest of the day.

When the adrenaline and shock wore off, I crashed hard. I wasn't looking forward to meeting with the police but there was no way out of it. If I didn't tell my story, Dominic might be set free and there was no way I'd allow that to happen. What he did to me I wouldn't wish on my worst enemy and from the sounds of it I was one of a long list of victims. He had to be stopped.

The next day, Detective Ambrose called and asked us to meet him at the station at two o'clock. We arrived a few minutes early, checked in with the officer at the front desk and notified them who we were there to see. They had us take a seat and not long after that Detectives Ambrose and Morton came out and led us back to a room with a table and four chairs. To me that room felt like the inside of a prison cell. There were no windows, the doors were made of steel and there was literally nothing else in it but the table and chairs. Daddy stood directly behind Stefan and me as we sat across from the detectives.

"Thank you, gentlemen, for coming in today. We appreciate your time. Since we last met more leads came in from other victims that Dominic abused. I think our mutual friend had something to do with that," Detective Ambrose said as he looked up at Daddy, but Daddy said nothing. "From there we set up a sting operation to lure him in, but he wasn't shopping for new clients, so to speak. His sights were set on the one he was obsessed with." Both the detectives stared at me.

"Me?" My voice shot up several octaves as I pointed at myself. "Why me?"

"Well, it appears you're the one that got away. He wasn't done with you that night and had Stefan not found you when he did you might not be here today." I stared up at Daddy and he was angry. His jaw was tightly clenched, and the muscle ticked.

"So, this whole thing yesterday was a setup? You put Riya's life in danger to lure Dominic in?" Daddy growled.

"Yes," Detective Morton admitted. "But Riya was never in danger. The crowd was filled with plain-clothed officers. We didn't want to alert you of the sting operation because we had it under control."

"Under control? He lunged at Riya with a knife in his hand," Daddy argued.

"Yes, but again, we had it under control. He got nowhere near Riya," Detective Morton argued.

"Had I not yanked Riya out of the way he would have reached him. He was that close," Daddy's voice escalated with every word he said.

"What-what do you need from us?" I asked. I just wanted to de-escalate this and get us out of here. We'd fill out whatever papers they needed, sign whatever they wanted, even point out Dominic in a lineup if I had to. We just needed to get out of here before Daddy blew up. He was pissed, I was upset, Stefan was silent, which was rare, so I knew he was upset. It was time to end this once and for all so we could move on with our lives.

"Riya, your recorded statement from when we first talked after the break-in will be submitted as evidence, but I need a written statement from each of you as to what you saw yesterday. You've already identified him so there's no need for a lineup. Let me get the forms and after you fill them out you can be on your way," Detective Ambrose said before he left the room.

"You're very lucky to be alive, Riya. Dominic has done terrible things to others. I'm not discounting what you went through and saying it's anything less than it was because it was horrible, and no one deserves to go through that. But had Stefan not found you when he did, we wouldn't be talking today." Detective Morton rose and followed his partner out, leaving the three of us alone. I didn't know what else to say, none of us did. A few minutes later Detective Ambrose came back in, and we gave our statements, handed them to him and left. He said he'd be in touch if he needed anything else. I hoped like hell the only time we heard from him was when he informed us that Dominic had been sentenced and sent to prison. End of story.

Chapter Thirteen

Jonovan

"Those spineless jackals. How dare they put my boys in danger? What the fuck were they thinking?" I yelled as I paced back and forth.

"Daddy," I heard Stefan say, so lost in my tirade I forgot where I was. "Are you okay? 'Cause you are kind of freaking us out and Titus is whining while he watches you."

I turned and stared right into the worried faces of my boys. That was enough to put things into perspective. It was over. Dominic was in jail and Riya was safe. "I'm so sorry, boys. I'm just," I ran my fingers through my hair and gave it a rough tug. The slight pain served as a reminder that we were still here. The boys and I were safe. I probably looked like a deranged psycho with my hair poking out in all directions. “They had no right to put you in danger.”

“Yeah, but would you have let them go through with their plan if they had told you first?” Stefan asked.

“Hell no. I would never grant a soul permission to put either of you in harm’s way,” I replied, far more forceful than need be. What I needed was a distraction that kept my mind busy. Or a stiff drink. Or both. Too bad I didn’t have a lawn to mow, that always worked when I was a kid.

“But their sting operation was successful,” Stefan reminded me. “They caught Dominic and he’s in jail.”

“They should’ve found somebody else to play the part and from the sounds of it there were many to choose from.” Why I kept up with the ridiculous argument I will never know. All it served to do was piss me off even more.

“Yeah, but it was me he wanted,” Riya whispered, and I dropped to the floor in front him. I couldn’t take the defeated tone of his voice.

“I can't risk losing either of you. You mean everything to me.” I couldn't take it anymore and for the first time in front of my boys I openly wept. The terror that coursed through me when I saw that knife wielded toward Riya, my first thought was to get in front of him but there wasn't enough time. I would lay down my life for these boys without thought, without regret. Instead, I grabbed him and yanked him out of the way. The detectives dove for Dominic just as I moved Riya, that knife was inches from my sweet Kitty. Afterward, I couldn't let him go. It was almost like if I did, he may have disappeared and then there'd be no more Riya in my life. Surviving wouldn't be an option after that.

We needed a break. The boys and I needed to get away.

"Boys, how would you like to go on vacation?" I asked and both looked at me like I had lost my mind, and perhaps I had. A bit of time at my parents' property up by the lake in Show Low was just what this family needed.

"Umm, what about our jobs?" Stefan said in a way that confirmed he thought I was crazy.

"Do you have any vacation time or...?" I left it up to them to decide. I already mentioned several times I was good with them not working and they always rebutted with they wanted to have their own money which I understood, though my finances were more than enough to support us.

"I'd like for us to go up to my parents' property for a few days and get away from the hectic mess our lives have become. Titus loves it up there, there's plenty of room for us and I think you boys would enjoy it. Lord knows my mother would be thrilled. You'll be coddled and fed like you've never been before. I don't think that woman ever learned to cook for two. I've heard my father complain about it more times than I could count." With each word I uttered the excitement at seeing my parents and them finally meeting the boys escalated. I knew they'd love them and the boys likewise. They may not understand our dynamic, but my parents were respectful of my lifestyle. The only thing they would care about was that we were happy.

"You want us to meet your parents?" Riya finally spoke.

"They've heard a lot about you, so I think it's time. What do you guys say?" They both shrugged. I wasn't sure if that was an I'm in or a let's just do it to shut the crazy man up.

"We've taken more time off since we started dating you than we have since we started working. I'm not sure what our bosses would say and it's kind of short notice. We're told we have to make time off requests at least two weeks in advance," Stefan, my voice of reason said, sounding much like the employee handbook I'm sure he'd read that in.

While they made their calls, I made mine. My mother squealed so loud I thought she'd burst my eardrum. "Mom, it's not that exciting, I swear." I tried to calm her, but she wouldn't have it. Instead, she rambled in Spanish and lost me. Why she never taught me her native language I'd never understand. My dad said he only got bits and pieces of it most of the time, but he loved my mother fiercely. But once she got going, he just sat back and let her get it all out then gave her a kiss and whatever tirade she was on ended. To this day they still looked at each other with cartoon hearts in their eyes. It drove me crazy as a kid, especially when they'd kiss and be all lovey dovey. To me then it was like *oh gross*, then I went through a phase where

I envied them. Now the love I felt for my boys rivaled theirs, at least in my heart it did.

Such a fool in love was I.

Ha, maybe I was a poet and didn't know it.

Nah, best not give up the day job.

After I hung up with my mother I reached out to my assistant. As of late, she'd taken over most of my tasks. Cell reception would be hit or miss in the mountains, but I could always drive over to the local coffee shop. If the need arose and I had to make a zoom call or something there was an option at least. I didn't know why I hadn't thought of taking the boys up north sooner. Pre-planning would've been key and made it a lot easier for Stefan and Riya. The urge to get away from the mess our lives had become when I knew it didn't need to be. Plus, I needed the boys to see normal because it sounded like all they'd known was chaos.

I'd just hung up with my assistant when the boys came into the office, neither of them appeared to be happy. "What's wrong, boys?"

"Well," Stefan began, "my boss said since nobody died that when I get back, he's writing me up."

"And mine told me I should consider finding a new place of employment," Riya added.

"Shit, I'm sorry, boys. We don't have to go." Riddled with guilt, it was selfish of me to ask this of them. But damn, was it wrong of me to want to take them away from all of this?

"Maybe it's not a bad idea for us to consider other options. We've been at these jobs forever and we've always worked to live, not necessarily lived to work. If that makes any sense," Stefan said.

"It does, and not to sound like a broken record but you boys do have options. You could go back to school or stay home and play with Titus all day. All that matters to me is that you're happy," I gave them my broken record speech for the umpteenth time.

"We know, Daddy," Riya said as he took a seat in my lap. I loved it when my little cuddle bug did that. "Maybe this trip will be the perfect time for us to really stop and think, something we've never been able to do before."

Well, now we were getting somewhere. "Do either of you like to fish?" I asked, recalling the great times my dad and I had. My old gear was stashed away in my parents' garage. Dad and I used to love to get up early on Sunday mornings and fish. The times we were lucky enough to catch anything, Mom would cook it for dinner that very night. There was nothing like dining on fish you caught with your own two hands. It was so much better than store bought.

"I don't think either of us have ever been. I know I haven't," Stefan replied and turned to Riya.

"Same," Riya added, "but I'm not touching worms and I'd feel terrible if I killed anything. Maybe it's not for me. Think I could just hang out with your mom?"

"My sweet, sensitive Kitty. Anything your heart desires. Same for you, Pup. If you guys don't want to fish that's fine. You could play alongside the lake, or skip rocks, or wander around the forest while Dad and I fish. Their property is surrounded by trees, it's absolutely breathtaking. I love being up there. There's a peaceful, Zen-like calm that comes over me. It's so much cooler up in the mountains temperature wise than down here in the valley.

"The wind whistles through the pines, the cool breeze that comes through the open windows while I sleep. Waking up to slightly chilled temps outside. I love to grab a cup of coffee, wrap myself up in a blanket and sit out on the porch and swing while I enjoy the silence. Titus entertains himself by chasing random bugs. Momma laughs at him and his nubby tail. That woman deserves the pedestal Dad and I have her up on, she is our queen."

"I'm sold." Stefan's voice snapped me from the daydream.

"I often thought of building on their property. They have fifteen acres and no neighbors in sight."

"Why haven't you?" Riya asked as he twisted his fingers through my beard.

"Well, I suppose it's because I never had anyone to share it with. This time when Dad mentions it, I might see it in a different light." I could already picture the three of us and Titus up there. If the boys enjoyed it as much as I did, I'd ask them what they thought. Maybe a move was what our future held. A new beginning for the three of us.

"I'll get the laundry started so we can pack," Riya said, and hopped off my lap. Right now, he was in a good frame of mind, but I feared what tonight may bring once he went to sleep.

"Daddy?" Stefan said. He peered into the hallway then moved closer to me and dropped his voice. "Can I talk to you about something?"

"Of course, love, anything." Stefan moved to the seat Riya had just vacated atop my lap. I absolutely loved this.

"When we first moved here, Riya's nightmares stopped so I thought maybe being with you helped, then last night happened," he fidgeted with the buttons on my shirt.

"You're worried about him?" I asked, though I knew the answer and was of the same frame of mind. Being the Daddy, I had to be the strong one for my boys. These two had been together for a long time so the words needed to come from him, not me.

"Yes. Do you think it might help if he talks to someone, like a professional someone?" he whispered like it was a dirty word.

"I do. Do you think he'd be open to us asking him or willing to consider it?" I'd thought of this earlier today and decided to wait and see if it happened again before broaching the subject. "Has this happened often?"

"Often enough. He'll go a couple of weeks with nothing then something triggers it and he'll have a few bad nights in a row. We don't have insurance and we couldn't pay for it out of pocket so I just took care of him as best I could," Stefan sniffed. My poor Stefan was hurting, consumed with worry for the man he loved.

I squeezed my sweet Pup. "You've been such a brave boy, taking care of Riya all by yourself. How can Daddy help?"

"Do you guys have any…" Riya popped his head in and asked. "Oh my God, that is too cute. Where's my phone? I want a picture of Pup on Daddy's lap," he flitted off in search of his phone which he'd likely find in his pocket.

Stefan moved, but I stopped him. "He'll be sad if he doesn't get his picture," I said with a kiss to the tip of Pup's nose. Seconds later, Riya reappeared.

"Okay, look at me," Riya said and snapped a couple of pictures.

"I have an idea, Kitten. Why don't you both sit on Daddy's lap, and I'll try to get a picture of the three of us?" I asked, Riya squealed and joined us. "On the count of three," I stretched my arm out as far as it could reach and did my best to get a clean shot. "One, two, three," I snapped a couple for them to pick through. "Text me the one you choose, and I'll set it as my screen saver."

"Yes, Daddy," they kissed my cheeks and hopped off and away. I guessed that was the end of our conversation for now but knowing Stefan and I were on the same page with this helped.

How did I get to be the luckiest man in the world?

Chapter Fourteen

Stefan

There was a part of me that was jealous Daddy had such wonderful parents when Riya and I hadn't had the same. What if they didn't like us or told Daddy to get rid of us? Did it even work that way? Our families threw us away so why wouldn't another?

"Ohhh, I love this song. Turn it up please, Stefan," Riya sang from the back seat. Daddy let us pick the music for the four-hour ride to his parents' house and Riya had a great time singing along. Even when he forgot the words it was cute as hell. It was wonderful to see him this carefree and happy, it was like a weight had been lifted when Dominic got arrested. I was surprised last night that he didn't have any nightmares. Daddy and I were on high alert, and fully anticipated it but nothing came. Maybe he got the closure he needed?

Daddy reached over and laced our fingers together. "You okay, Pup?" I didn't want to be the one to ruin the mood in the car, so I nodded and shoved my fears aside. Daddy lifted my hand and pressed his lips to my knuckles. "I hope you know I'm here for you and I love you."

"I do and I love you, too." Daddy had a way of making things better, I just needed to get out of my own head because right now it wasn't a good place to be. Riya and I had a wonderful life with Daddy and I was determined to not ruin it. The three of us together were perfect, each personality offset the other and all the pieces clicked into place. He was the Daddy I dreamed of, and Riya and I loved him with all our hearts.

"Let's stop for lunch in Payson and stretch our legs. Sound good, boys?" Daddy asked.

"Yes, I'm starving," Riya sang his response like lyrics to a song. He really didn't have a bad voice though his dancing could use some work. Ha, who was I kidding? I had two left feet and was lucky I could walk and chew gum at the same time.

We pulled into a diner Daddy found and stretched our legs and backs the second we got out of the truck. "This is my first road trip and I'm having a blast," Riya announced as he spun around in the parking lot.

"Did you eat a gallon of sugar before we left?" I teased him.

"Oh, ha-ha. I'm just excited is all," Riya stuck his tongue out at me and made Daddy laugh.

"I'm glad you're having fun, Kitten, now let's get you fed," Daddy said as he grabbed Titus's leash. "I like this place, it's pet friendly. Titus and I have been here a few times."

The hostess seated us in a booth that overlooked the main street. I'd always enjoyed watching cars drive by in the hustle and bustle of people on their way somewhere. Many times, I'd make up stories in my head. *There goes Mary, off to pick up her son from band practice. Maybe they'll stop for ice cream before they go home and feed the dog.* Just silly things to pass the long days and nights. I spent so much time alone as a child that my imagination was my only friend. I'd wander around, find somewhere to sit and people watch. Then I'd sneak back into the house and go to sleep only to do it all over again the next day. I didn't like being home, it wasn't a safe place for me.

"Pup, are you okay?" Daddy asked again, Riya had just gone off to the restroom and the hostess dropped off a bowl of water and a treat for Titus.

"Yes. No. I don't know. Just thinking about a bunch of stuff I probably shouldn't be," I admitted, wadding the straw wrapper into a ball.

"Like what?" Daddy asked.

"It's stupid, really." He'd think I was such a dork if he knew my thoughts.

"There isn't anything stupid about you, Stefan." Daddy was very nice. How could I continue to deny him the answers he sought when he genuinely cared?

"Just remembered how I used to spend my time while I tried to stay away from home for as long as I could," I answered honestly. The one thing Daddy couldn't stand was lying, and I didn't feel good doing it as it was.

"And how was that?"

"I'd get up before anyone else. I didn't want to give them the chance to...well, let me just say that I needed to stay away from them. All of them," I paused. "I'd hurry up and eat if I could find something edible and then I'd stay gone until it got dark and sneak back in and hide in my room, and then do it all over again the next day." Daddy squeezed my knee and I continued. "I'd people watch from places I hid behind and make up stories in my head about them. It was stupid."

"I don't think it's stupid at all. Did you ever write any of them down?" he asked.

"No, they were really, really dumb." Even if I had written them down and the wrong person found them it would've been one more thing they'd make fun of me for.

"I think we should get you a journal and some pens. You can write down your thoughts, stories, poems, whatever you want. Who knows, maybe someday you could turn them into best-selling novels," Daddy said, far too happily. If I didn't know any better, I'd think this was his dream with as excited as he was. Heck, maybe it was. Riya and I never pried into Daddy's life or past when maybe we should've. Great, now I felt like a horrible boyfriend.

"Who'd want to buy anything from me?" I scoffed.

"I'd read anything you write," Riya said as he slid into the booth beside me and kissed my cheek. "I love you and I think you're wonderful."

"So, there you have it, Riya has spoken," Daddy winked at him, and Riya beamed.

"I don't know," I shrugged it off though I couldn't deny the idea of having a journal made me happy. Sometimes you just needed to get the thoughts out of your head and that was a safe way to do it. Maybe writing could turn out to be my kind of therapy.

We finished eating and got back in the truck. Daddy merged into traffic and announced, "We have one more stop to make before we hit the highway." A few minutes later, he pulled into the parking lot of a store. "This will do. Come on, boys." He rolled down the window just enough for Titus to stick his head out. "We'll be back in a minute, Titus. Keep an eye on the truck." Titus barked like he knew what Daddy said. "It's nice and cool today so he'll be more than comfortable."

Daddy grabbed a cart, and we trailed behind him. "If you see any snacks you want, grab them." We found a few things but stayed away from anything refrigerated or frozen since it wouldn't last the remaining two hours, and we didn't bring an ice chest. Daddy insisted on walking up and down every aisle, thankfully this wasn't a large store like we were used to in the valley. Riya was antsy and wanted us both to hurry up. He was super excited to meet Daddy's family. "Aha, here we are," Daddy announced as we walked down the school supply aisle. "Why don't you each pick something out." He wrapped his arm around me and kissed the top of my head. "They have a great selection of notebooks and pens."

That giddy feeling Riya had ever since we woke up hit me full force as I flipped through every single one they had. Eventually I landed on a notebook with a tiny lock and key with a cute baby dragon on the cover and a pack of pens with six different colors. Riya chose an animal coloring book and crayons. "Thank you, Daddy," we both said as we hugged him.

"You are very welcome, my sweet boys. Now, let's go pay and get back in the car before Titus eats the seats," Daddy teased. A few minutes later we were loaded up and back on the road. Riya again chose the back seat because he enjoyed sitting with Titus. He really loved that dog, as did I but I caught him sneaking Titus extra treats when Daddy wasn't looking. This was the life we were meant to have, and I owed whatever gods there may be many thanks for bringing Daddy to us.

After we passed through Show Low and got off the highway, we drove onto a long, winding dirt road. I didn't think it would ever end and then out of the blue appeared the cutest log cabin engulfed in all sorts of trees. Titus started barking before Daddy even had the truck in park and the front screen burst open and out came one very excited woman waving at us.

"Momma!" Daddy called out as he ran and picked her up. She protested though it fell on deaf ears, plus her giggling gave away how happy she was to see him.

"Mijo, put me down so I can meet your boys," she said. Daddy gave her one last squeeze and placed her on her feet. "So cute you are," she patted our cheeks. "Come, come, I feed you." She took our hands and led us toward the house. We glanced back over our shoulders at Daddy who smiled and waved as he embraced the man who silently stood nearby.

Daddy explained this wasn't his childhood home during the ride up. He said that when his parents retired, they sold their house in Phoenix and moved up here. There were family photos everywhere. "Look at little Jonovan," she pointed to one of his grade school pictures. "Good thing he grew out of that phase."

"I heard that, Momma," Daddy called from the other room.

"I didn't whisper," she loudly replied to make sure he heard. I'd known this woman all of five minutes and I loved her already. "We need a picture of you three, I'll have Mario take one with his camera phone.

"Here, sit," she pointed to the dining table and sat a plate of cookies down. "Milk or coffee?"

"Milk, please, Mrs. Duarte," I replied.

"I don't know who this Mrs. lady is, but you call me Momma," she said in a stern voice that was somehow still filled with love. "Yes?"

"Okay, Momma," Riya chimed in. He was all over this family stuff. I guess I could learn a thing or two from him today. I just needed to learn to let go.

A few minutes later, Daddy and his father walked in. "Where are my cookies, Momma?" Daddy teased her.

"Sit. Eat," she ushered him toward a chair.

"Riya, Stefan, I'm Mario, Jonovan's father," Mario said. Riya and I stood and shook his hand. "Welcome. I see my bride was already bossing you around?" He winked, knowing full well that would get a rise out of her.

"Everybody knows who wears the pants in this family," she proudly announced and tapped her finger on the table for emphasis. Mario laughed and kissed her. God, they were adorable.

“My boy never brought anybody home except for his friend Steve who we've met a couple of times. But nobody he ever dated,” Momma said as she sat down with a cup of coffee in hand. “This is important. You are important to him.”

“Gee thanks, Momma. First you out me and it doesn’t even come with coffee for me,” Daddy teased and rolled his eyes but grinned the entire time. “I wonder what you’ll do next?”

“You know where the coffee is, you can get it yourself,” she clicked her tongue at him. “Does my Jonovan cook for you boys? I taught him everything he knows in the kitchen so don't ever let him tell you he can't cook because he can.”

“Da-err, Jonovan,” Riya quickly corrected himself, “is a good cook. He makes dinner almost every night. Stefan and I can barely boil water.”

Mario started laughing. “We may not understand your lifestyle, but it is yours. If you wish to call Jonovan Daddy while you're here, go right ahead, just don't be surprised if I turn around and respond. It'll take me a bit to get used to not being the daddy around here.” Riya and my head pivoted so fast toward our Daddy, our eyes wide open as we waited for his reaction.

“I told you both before, you can call me Daddy in public, or private, or you can call me Jonovan. Whatever you feel most comfortable with. I would never force you to say or do anything you didn't want to," Daddy replied.

"Thanks, Daddy," Riya said. I enjoyed the playful banter between Daddy's family. They truly loved one other. To me, this was how a family should be.

"Come, Jonovan," Mario said as he stood. "Let's bring your things in and see where that crazy dog of yours got off to."

Momma started cracking up. "Have you seen his little tail?" She clicked her tongue again. "It's sad that they cut it off but it's funny to watch it go when he gets excited. It just goes *thump, thump, thump* in the air." She barely got the last word out before she burst into a fit of giggles. Riya and I laughed along with her, though I wasn't sure if it was due to the visual her words conjured or her infectious laughter.

"Psst, boys," Daddy poked his head into the kitchen area. "Follow me." He led us up the stairs where there were two bedrooms and a bathroom. "Downstairs is where my parents' room is. When they built this house, they put the master suite down there. Momma didn't want to deal with stairs anymore. We have our choice of rooms, which do you prefer?"

We peeked inside both. "Those aren't king-sized beds, Daddy. How are we gonna fit?" I asked. At home we had a ginormous king-sized bed that we fit comfortably in.

"We'll make it work, Pup." Titus bounded up the stairs. "We'll have to keep an eye on him, he likes to chase squirrels and I'm afraid of what would happen if he ever caught one," Daddy said, and I cringed. That was an image I could definitely do without. "Tomorrow morning Dad and I are going fishing. Do you guys want to come with, or do you want to stay here with Momma?"

"How far is it to the lake?" Riya asked. "Not that I want to fish but I would like to go exploring. Oh, and what time are you going?"

My boys were not early risers. "Dad and I will be up and casting our lines before the sun rises. There's a trail right outside the cabin to the right. If you follow it, it will lead you straight down to the lake so if you get up and we're not here, walk down and meet us. If you decide to wander around, don't go too far unless you're on one of the paths because you will get lost. Trust me, I've done that a time or two."

"Well, you pick the room, Daddy," Riya said. "As long as I'm snuggled up between you and Stefan I can sleep anywhere." He grabbed his bag, skipped off into one of the rooms and started unpacking. So much for Daddy choosing. I loved this silly side of Riya. I'd honestly never seen him like this and it was wonderful. Maybe Daddy was right, a vacation was just what we needed.

Chapter Fifteen

Riya

When you look up the definition of *happy* in the dictionary it says, *see Riya Cox*.

Just kidding, but that's how I felt now that I had found my furrever home. Correction, now that *we* found our furrever home. Two wayward souls, a lonely pup and a scaredy cat, finally had a family. *We* belonged. You didn't need to share DNA to be a family, the only ingredient required was a heart. Daddy and his family had enough room in theirs for us and I was beyond grateful.

Daddy's family had been nothing but wonderful to us the whole time we'd been there. Momma showed us how to cook. We made tamales and homemade tortillas. Everything was wonderful and she didn't get mad whenever I messed up. She just made me start over again so I could remember how to do it right. In the end I was no master chef by any means, but at least I understood the words in a recipe now. She was patient and laughed when I did something silly. Stefan popped in and out of the kitchen sneaking bites of our treats and then was off again. Mostly, being the nature of the pup he was, he chased Titus around or went down to the lake and watched Daddy and Mario fish. This place was my version of heaven and we each had our own little slice to make our own.

Sadly, our last night here had come and I for one wasn't looking forward to going home. Not that home was bad, it was actually the opposite. I loved our life with Daddy, but it was calm and peaceful up here in the mountains, like no one else in the world existed outside of us five and Titus. No hustle and bustle of the city, no worry about how we were gonna get from one place to another. I knew technically we didn't have to worry about that anymore because Daddy took us wherever we needed to go. Still, sometimes I felt guilty, like he did too much, but he said that's what Daddies did for their boys, and it made Daddy happy to be able to do that for us. Who was I to argue with Daddy logic?

Daddy had been patient with me and never asked for or even hinted at having anal sex. He or Stefan or sometimes both would make sure I orgasmed when they had sex, just not through penetration. Watching them together was such a turn on and many times I almost gave in, but something held me back. Maybe it just wasn't the right time or place. I knew that was my problem to work on, and I was, though I hadn't seen a therapist yet. I probably should. I'd talk to Daddy and Stefan about it when we got home. For now, I was working on making myself understand that Daddy wasn't Dominic. Daddy wouldn't hurt me, and Daddy would stop if I said to.

But was I mentally ready for sex? Penetrative sex that was?

What happened if we got started and I freaked out, or started crying, or did something stupid? I would feel like such a fool, like I let Daddy down even though I knew he wouldn't see it that way. It was just my fear taking control when I needed to be the one in charge. Fear should not lead me. The online research and various articles I'd read about people who experienced similar traumatic situations like mine had been helpful. I joined online chat groups and of course, many of them suggested I find a local therapy group. So far, I'd found the forums to be insightful without doing face-to-face meetings. That was another huge hurdle for me, opening up to strangers. What would people think when they saw me, and I shared my story? Would they say I was young and stupid? That I put myself in harm's way? Maybe I did, but that still didn't give

Dominic the right to do what he did to me. People online couldn't see me. It was a safe way to share my thoughts and fears. In person, I wasn't sure I'd be able to do it.

Well, I'd never know until I tried, and I really wanted to try with Daddy.

Today I decided to go down to the lake and watch Daddy and Mario fish. About halfway around the other side where it wouldn't disturb the fish near Daddy and Mario, Stefan threw a stick out into the water for Titus, and he loved going after it. He'd get a running start and take off, dive into the water and bring it back, and do it all over again. Stefan barked back and forth with Titus like they were carrying on a conversation. He was becoming more like his Pup persona with every passing day, and I enjoyed watching his transformation.

Camped out on the blanket I brought with me not far from Daddy I'd switch from reading to watching the pups play, to listening to Daddy and Mario talk, all while perched beneath the pine tree canopy. The sun peaked through as the greenery allowed and the whole scene filled me with a peaceful tranquility I'd never felt before. There was nothing better than lying here with book in hand, and taking all this wonder in. What a perfect day, too bad it was our last one.

"Whatcha reading?" Stefan asked as he plopped down on the blanket beside me. Titus took that moment to shake the water off.

"Yuck," I complained, and shook the book to free it of the vile droplets. "Now we all smell like lake water."

Stefan giggled, "Wow, someone's grouchy."

I huffed. "Not grouchy, just bummed."

Daddy turned in his camping chair to face us, "What's wrong, Kitty?"

I slid the bookmark between the pages and sat the book down. "I love it here. Do we really have to leave?"

Daddy handed his fishing pole to Mario and took a seat on the blanket beside us. "I'm sorry, love, we do." I sighed, defeated, and my shoulders drooped. "But," my head popped up at the single word that held so much hope for me. "I can promise we will come up here more often. We have lives to tend to at home, job situations to figure out. Maybe we could have one long weekend a month that we came to visit. Would that be a fair compromise?"

Stefan and I tackled Daddy, Titus ran circles around us and barked like mad. "Yes, Daddy!"

"All right, now that we've scared the fish away," Daddy began and then he stole a kiss. "Let's pick up our things and head back to the house."

Knowing this wasn't a once a year or an only on special occasions retreat made all the difference for me. It was a promise, a plan, something solid that said Daddy wasn't letting us go. Did I really think he would? Well, not so much anymore but there was always that niggling negative voice in the back of my mind that told me I'd never be worthy of him. With each passing day, that voice began to fade but it was never gone.

For the rest of the afternoon, we played board games together as a family. Daddy and Mario played a card game called War that was far too intense for me but super fun to watch as they tried to best each other. Momma brought out snacks and would sneak a peek at Mario's cards and silently try to tell Daddy what he had but Mario caught her each time. At one point he grabbed her around the waist and pulled her onto his lap. She protested, though not hard enough and when he kissed her, her eyes lit up like it was the first time all over again. That's the love I'd always read about but didn't believe it was possible, or real. Having watched those two still in love after forty years of marriage, I now believed it was possible and Stefan and I had found it with our Daddy.

The three of us took turns showering, I was the last one to go in. I needed to take my time and ensure I was ready not only physically, but mentally as well. I really wanted to share this with Daddy and Stefan, the part of me I'd held back for far too long, and tonight was the perfect night.

I walked into the room, shut the door behind me and crawled into place between them. "Um, Daddy?"

"Yes, Kitten?"

"Do you want to...? I mean, would you...? Ugh, I'm blowing this," I muttered.

"Are you okay, Riya?" Stefan asked.

Come on, Riya, you're a big boy and these two men love you with their whole hearts.

"Daddy, would you make love to me?" I blurted out and chewed my bottom lip while I waited for his answer.

"My sweet Kitten," Daddy said as he slid his knuckles along my cheeks in soothing strokes. "I'd love nothing more, but are you certain that's what you want?"

I nodded but knew Daddy would want a verbal reply for such a big request. "Yes, Daddy, I am."

Kissing.

Daddy's lips on mine were like heaven.

Making love always began with kissing.

And Daddy and Stefan loved me.

So many nights the three of us fell asleep while kissing and talking. I'm sure some people thought us moving in with Daddy as fast as we had was bad. But it wasn't. Nothing was rushed, Daddy had been the most patient man on the planet, and he made sure that Stefan and I were taken care of, and our needs were met. Even if his weren't always, he never complained.

Tonight, like so many others, it all started with a kiss.

Together they undressed me, then themselves. I loved being taken care of and coddled. "I love you, sweet boy," Daddy said to me, his eyes never leaving mine. The truth of his words were clear as anything in his soft gaze.

"I love you, too, Daddy. And I love you, Stefan," I replied.

"Love you, Riya," Stefan said, and snatched another kiss before his lips moved along my jaw, a gentle kiss placed beneath my ear, triggering a ticklish spot.

Daddy did the same, though he continued down my left side while Stefan stopped to toy with my nipples. They were super sensitive and a straight shot to my cock which was already painfully hard. I'd had plenty of orgasms while we'd been here but how I really wanted to come was with Daddy inside me and I'd been thinking about it all day. Now I knew how Stefan felt the first night he wanted Daddy to claim him.

They took turns whispering sweet words of encouragement and love to me. I'd never felt so cherished, so beautiful, so loved in all my life. Gently, Daddy parted my legs and took his place between them and lifted my hips. "I've wanted to taste you for so long, sweet boy." He pressed his lips to the inside of my thigh and trailed them up to my rim. He ran his tongue upward from my taint to balls and back down again.

"Oh, Daddy," I moaned. No one had ever performed such an intimate act on me. It was...it was...mind numbing to the point I could barely string two words together. Between Daddy's magical lips and the dual sensation of Stefan sucking my nipples while he stroked my cock, I was overloaded. When Daddy's tongue breached my hole, that was it. "Daddy. Stefan. Gonna. Gonna." That was all the warning they got before I came. Stefan licked my stomach clean, then his hand, and cleared away every last drop.

Stefan moved up alongside me. "Taste yourself," he said, and slid his tongue inside my mouth. Could this night get any hotter? From the way they cherished every inch of me to Stefan licking away the remnants of my orgasm, it was so much more than I'd dreamed possible. My dick took notice, and it wouldn't be long before he was back in the game.

"Daddy, fuck Stefan, please," I panted, and Daddy sat up.

"But I thought?" he said with a sad look on his face.

"You two together gets me all kinds of hot and I want to come again when you're inside me," I explained. "I'm not done, just trying to catch my breath. What you guys did to me was amazing."

Daddy kissed me. "Absolutely, sweet boy." He grabbed the lube, but we'd forgone condoms a while back after we all got tested, and Daddy and Stefan had gone bareback several times since then. I remember how relieved I was when we got our test results. After Dominic, I should've gone straight to the clinic to be tested but I was too embarrassed to step foot inside and risk having to admit what had happened. I got lucky, that's for sure.

Stefan assumed the position and hovered over me so he could kiss me while Daddy's fingers opened him. "This feels so good, Riya. Daddy's the best at this, so gentle and he knows just where…" His eyes rolled back, and he moaned. "Just where to touch."

"Are you ready, sweet Pup?" Daddy asked, Stefan wiggled his ass in response. Daddy spanked him and Stefan yelped. "Hold still, Pup." Stefan loved it when Daddy spanked him during adult playtime. Hell, he loved in while in pup headspace, too. It wasn't for me, though, but I didn't mind watching Stefan get off on it.

Stefan's mouth consumed mine as Daddy entered him. I swallowed his every moan, and patiently waited my turn. I knew it would hurt given how long it had been for me, but the look of ecstasy on Stefan's face had me nearly begging to switch places. But I was patient, and I would wait. Besides, I'd already come once so it was Stefan's turn to now.

"Don't come inside him, Daddy," I called out. "Save it for me, please."

"I'll do my best, Kitten," Daddy nearly growled in that sexy way he does.

"Watching Riya come undone like he did, it won't take long for me," Stefan added. I reached up and began to stroke him. I knew the dual stimulation would make him come faster and then I'd get my turn.

Stefan didn't know which way to fuck, back toward Daddy or forward into my fist. His body was at odds chasing both sides and he was getting growly which made me laugh. Daddy pounded harder, and I stroked faster.

"Jesus," Stefan panted. Sweat beaded on his forehead. "Right," before he could say *there*, he thrust forward into my hand, his dick pulsed, and he came. Daddy stilled and when Stefan collapsed, he slid out.

"Give me a sec," Stefan said, as he held up a hand. Daddy hopped up and went into the bathroom and returned with a wet rag. After he'd cleaned himself and my stomach off, Stefan rolled over.

"Do you want to be up on all fours or facing me?" Daddy asked me.

"Facing you, if that's okay?" I asked.

"That is more than okay. I would love to stare into your beautiful eyes as I make love to you." Daddy said the sweetest things. He took extra time getting me ready, doing everything he could to ensure it wouldn't hurt as much. His sturdy fingers massaged my opening, in and out. I was in heaven already and he wasn't even inside me. "Are you ready, my sweet Kitten?"

"Yes, Daddy."

Daddy lifted my legs and pressed the tip of his cock to my hole while Stefan lay beside me whispering how hot it was watching Daddy finger me, how great I was doing and how much they loved me. Stefan's fingertips glided along my naked flesh, leaving a wake of goosebumps. These two men owned me on every level. As Daddy slid inside, my eyes filled with tears. "Riya, are you okay? Do you need me to stop?"

"These are happy tears, Daddy."

Slowly, Daddy made love to me. Long, deep thrusts as his cock repeatedly drug across that sweet spot. The love reflected in his gaze was what sent me careening over the edge. "Oh Daddy," I cried out and the tears fell. "Daddy. Daddy. Daddy," I chanted through my orgasm.

Daddy thrust harder, faster, once, twice, as he chased his own release. On the last thrust he pressed in as far as he could go and on the third time he held in place as he came inside me. "My sweet boys," he called out as he filled me. Marked me. Made me his as he had done to Stefan. We were his boys, no one else's. There would never be another Daddy for me.

"Thank you, Daddy," I said when he was finished.

He brushed the sweat-soaked hair from my forehead. "For what, sweet boy?"

"For being patient with me. For being my, "I glanced over at Stefan, "I mean our Daddy. For being you."

"You never need to thank me for that, sweet Kitten. I belong to you and Pup forever more."

Epilogue

Jonovan

Two years later

"Daddy, I can't believe you kept this from us all this time," Stefan protested, arms crossed menacingly across his chest. He was the sweetest little pouter, I swear.

"Keep what from you? The windows are covered so you can't see in, but you've seen the outside all along," I shook my head at his silliness.

"Gah," Riya murmured and threw his hands up. "Duh, and now we want to see the inside."

Wow, my boys barely held it together while waiting for the grand unveiling of the cabin my father and some of my crew had been working on for the last eight months for us. It didn't take long after our first visit to decide this was where we'd rather be, but that dream took a lot of time and money to bring to fruition. It was important everything be just right for my Pup and Kitty.

"All right, go get Momma and we'll let you inside," I rolled my eyes for effect and knew that would get them moving.

"I saw that," Stefan hollered over his shoulder at me, though it didn't slow him down any. They'd already taken off and sprinted toward my parents' cabin before I'd finished speaking. No sooner had they left when I spotted them coming around the bend with Momma in tow. They hadn't even given her time to take her apron off. Good lord, was she still in her slippers?

"Boys, you didn't let her put her shoes on first?" I scolded, though jokingly. They stopped, glanced down at her feet and then right back up at me. The sheepish grins on their faces said it all. "All right, where's Titus?" I said just as he darted out of the bushes and straight inside our cabin.

"Titus!" both boys yelled and took off after him.

Well, so much for any sort of ribbon cutting ceremony...

"You have your hands full, son," Dad said with a pat to my back. "Better go see what they're getting into."

The man had no idea the mischief these too could bring. And I loved every single moment of it.

I shook my head and went in search of two very naughty boys. When I stepped inside, they hadn't made it very far and stood in the middle of the room and stared up at the expansive twenty-four-foot-high log cabin ceiling while they slowly spun. Titus was in super sleuth mode, sniffing every square inch of the new place and gave it the once over while he dotted everything with his smushy snout. And likely left behind Boxer bogies, too. I cringed, not at all thrilled about the prospect of wiping his snot off our new stuff.

"So, boys, what do you think?" I asked and their spinning halted.

"Whoa," Stefan replied. "How'd you get the ceiling fan way up there?" He pointed to the highest point in the roof.

"Magic," I replied in lieu of stating the obvious.

"Momma, Momma, Momma," Riya chanted as she stepped inside. "Have you seen this ginormous kitchen? Imagine all the tamales we could make in here!"

Momma sighed but Dad laughed. "Ah, you laugh now but just you wait," she warned Dad. Many times over the years she'd used that empty threat but it never had an ending. Wait for what exactly was what I always wondered.

Riya grabbed her by the hand and led her to the kitchen. Those two were the best of friends now and I loved it. I thought they each found a need filled by the another.

My mother's need to take care of someone, or multiple someone's, and Riya's need for a motherly figure. It was a beautiful relationship to watch bloom. She adored Stefan and he likewise, but he was more of a free spirit and enjoyed chasing bugs and woodland creatures alongside Titus.

"Is that a real fireplace?" Stefan asked and pointed to the floor-to-ceiling river rock structure that I nearly lost several fingers putting together when I caught them between two of the large stones. "Yes, it is. Have you ever had one?"

"No, I grew up in Phoenix. There's not much use for one when it's a hundred degrees year-round," Stefan replied. The boy wasn't wrong but up here during the winter months I envisioned us curled up under blankets, sipping hot cocoa while enjoying the crackling fire. Making love in front of it until the wee hours of the morning was one dream I looked very forward to fulfilling.

"It's massive," Stefan said as he ran his hands along it. "Where did you find these huge rocks?"

"A nearby rock quarry. There are tons of quarries all over the state." That wasn't an understatement. Not when you lived in the desert and the cities actually paid you to put rock in your yard instead of grass. Up here in the northern part of Arizona, grass was the norm due to all the inclement weather the area received.

"The first floor has a spare bedroom and bathroom along with a special room for Pup and Kitty," I teased.

Their eyes widened as they abandoned their current stations and bolted in that direction.

They opened the door, and my ears were greeted with another round of wows and Riya's excited squeal. The room wasn't carpeted with a plush carpet as the guest and master bedrooms were but instead, we laid down an indoor-outdoor carpeting with foam flooring pieces that interlocked in primary colors on top so it wouldn't be as hard on their knees when they played. They'd still have their kneepads and gloves on most of the time, but this would give their bodies a bit more added protection.

As we walked in on the left-hand side, there was a row of hooks that their gear hung from. Along the back wall there was a basket of dog toys, and another with cat toys in it. A human-sized scratching post that Riya could climb on. I made sure the base was heavily weighted and structured as to not tip over, and a pretend fire hydrant and tree was there for Stefan's pup to enjoy. Anything else they came up with could be purchased and added as I made sure there was plenty of room for growth.

"Daddy, this is amazing," Riya said as he squeezed my midsection in a tight hug.

"I couldn't agree more," Stefan added.

"Maybe sometime Steve and his koala can come and play. The spare bedroom across the hall would be perfect for them and they could have private playtime as well." Steve found a pet of his own and from time to time the boys would play with Timothy the koala both at the club as well as at our house in Phoenix.

"That's a great idea, Daddy," Stefan cheerfully replied as he dug through the bin of pup toys and tossed them all over the place.

"Come on, boys. Let me show you our bedroom." I was excited for this, and I hoped they liked what I had designed for us.

"Where does the door at the top of the stairs go?" Riya asked.

"The entire second floor is our bedroom," I replied. The boys ran up the stairs and straight inside with Titus hot on their heels. I entered into another round of wows.

The new king-sized bed sitting in the center of the room had a massive wrought iron headboard. A walk-in closet was to the right, and to the left was one of the biggest bathrooms my team had ever constructed.

"This shower is like a car wash for humans," Stefan's voice echoed from inside the tiled room. "Three waterfall shower heads."

"Yes, for the three men who live here. No more separate showers in tiny stalls for this family," I replied. Though the shower in the Phoenix house did fit the three of us, it didn't hold a candle to this massive car wash as Stefan had called it.

"The bathtub looks like the jacuzzi at our old apartment," Riya said. "Just without the nasty floaties and film on top." I cringed at his visual.

"Yes, the tub was also built for three and has jets like a jacuzzi." I did something out of the norm, and instead of two sinks and vanities, I put in three separate ones so we each had our own private bathroom storage spaces. The toilet itself was in a separate water closet. I preferred that then whomever had to take care of business wasn't disturbed while another showered or got ready. Soon enough we'd be living up here more than down in the valley so the need to ensure the three of us were comfortable was of the utmost importance. The fifty-gallon hot water heater would be earning its keep for sure.

"So, boys, what do you think?" I knew they'd love it, but the unsure Daddy inside craved confirmation.

"We love it!" they said, as they tackled me to the bed.

"There's something else I need to show you." My parents knew what came next, so they quietly shut the door and left the boys and I alone. I reached into my pocket and pulled out three matching titanium bands. "I know we can't be legally married, but I want to spend the rest of my life with you both. Will you, Pup and Kitty, be my life partners?" I opened my hand so they could see what it held.

"Oh my god," Riya said as he covered his face.

"Daddy?" Stefan whispered. "You want us like, forever?"

"Furrever, sweet boy. I want my Pup and my Kitten in their furrever home with me. What do you say?" I again asked.

"Yes!" they yelled at the same time and held their hands out. I slid their rings on and then together, they put mine in place.

"Furrever," Riya said.

"Furrever," Stefan added.

"Furrever, my loves."

About the Author

TL Travis is an award-winning published author of LGBTQIA+ contemporary and paranormal romance and erotic musings that have earned "Best-Selling Author" flags in the US as well as Internationally.

By day she and her team of mild-mannered maintenance techs are ridding the world of those pesky broken things. In her free time, TL enjoys catching up with her family, attending concerts, wine tasting, and traveling.

Other books by TL Travis

The Social Sinners Series:

Boxset:

https://books2read.com/SSWorldTour

Behind the Lights, 1

MM Coming of Age Rockstar Romance

In the Shadows,2

MM Rockstar Hurt/Comfort Romance

A Heart Divided, 3

MMMM Rockstar Romance

Beyond the Curtain, 4

MM BDSM Hurt/Comfort PTSD Rockstar Romance

After the Final Curtain, 5

MM BDSM Rockstar Romance

Bonus Story

Diamond& Easton's Vegas Elopement

MM Rockstar Romance

Maiden Voyage Series:

Boxset

Ryder's Guardian, 1

MM Rockstar Bodyguard Romance

Derek's Destiny, 2

MM Rockstar Teacher Romance

Jaxson's Nemesis, 3

MM Enemies to lovers Rockstar Romance

Shadow's Light, 4

MM Rockstar Hurt/Comfort Second Chance Romance

Bonus Story

Claiming the Guardian

MM Rockstar Bodyguard Romance

Embrace The Fear (ETF) Series:

Embrace the Fear World Tour: Complete Collection

Rhone'sRebel, 1

MM Hurt/Comfort Rockstar Romance

David's Disaster, 2

MM Daddy-boy Hurt/Comfort Rockstar Romance

Seltzer'sTaylor, 3

MM Rockstar Romance

His Final Chase, 4

MM Rockstar Daddy-Little Romance

Chaotic Abyss Series

Strike a Chord, 1

MM Rockstar Second Chance Romance

Higher Notes, 2

MMM Rockstar Bodyguard Romance

Daddies and their Littles

When Daddy Hurts

MM Daddy-Little Hurt/Comfort Romance

A Little Christmas: Jacob

MM Daddy-Little Hurt/Comfort Holiday Romance

A Little Christmas: Orion's Secret

MM Daddy-Little Hurt/Comfort Holiday Romance

A Little Christmas 3: Ralphie

MM Daddy-Little Hurt/Comfort Holiday Romance

Two Daddies for Henry

MMM Daddy Hurt/Comfort Found Family Romance

A Little's Valentine's Party: Featuring Jacob & Orion

Daddy's Little Dreamer

Lactin Brotherhood Series

Littles in the Wild

Pride Camp 2025

Mommies and their Littles

Mommy Calls Me Princess

Sapphic

Girl Crush

FF Sapphic Romance/ 1 MF scene

What Works For Us

FF Over 40 Erotic Novelette

Menotte avec toi (Handcuffed with you)

Co-author novel with Layla Dorine

FF BDSM club

Pet Play

Pick Us, Daddy

Pride Pet Play 2023 Series

https://books2read.com/PPP2023

Ahoy Daddy!

Pride Cruise 2024 Series

MM Daddy Romance

Daddies:

Pints 'n Pool

Foggy Basin Season 1

MM Daddy Small Town Romance

Pints 'n Pool Holiday

A Foggy Basin Short Story

Finding Ash

Foggy Basin Season 2

A Daddy for Christmas 1: Brighton

MM Daddy Holiday Romance

A Daddy for Christmas 2: Jobe

MM Daddy Holiday Romance

Fantasy

Mpreg/Bear Shifter:

Naughty Elf: Twinkle: M/M Mpreg Shifter Christmas Romance

https://books2read.com/TlTwinkle

Dragon Shifters:

From Authors Layla Dorine & TL Travis

Primordial Protectors Series

Amethyst Storms

Emerald Waves

Infernal Ruby

Sapphire Seas

Venomous Topaz

Standalone novels:

Heat

MM Small Town Coming of Age Bear Bottom Romance

See Me

MM Hurt/Comfort Enemies to Lovers Body Positive/Disfigurement Romance

Greyson Fox Saga (each can be read as a standalone):

Greyson Fox

MM Erotic May/December Age-Gap First Time Coming of Age Romance

Forgive Me Father

MM Coming of Age Hurt/Comfort Rent-a-boy Romance

Stand-alone novelette's/novella's:

Summer Boy

MM Small Town First-Time Coming of Age Demisexual Romance

Rules of the Game

MM Erotic Workplace Romance

Coffee, Tea or Me?

MM Contemporary Romance

Snowed In With You

MM Contemporary Second Chance Holiday Romance

Paranormal Romance:

The Sebastian Chronicles

Historical Paranormal Erotic Romance

(Includes all 5 stories listed below)

Sebastian, The Beginning

MF Historical Paranormal Erotica

My Servant, My Lover

MF/MM Historical Paranormal Erotica

Wealthy Ménage

MF/MM/MFM/Ménage Historical Paranormal Erotica

Prohibition Inhibitions

MF/MM/MMF/MFM/BDSM Historical Paranormal Erotica

The Tryst - Chronicle Finale

MM Paranormal Erotic Romance

Pity the Living, Not the Dead

MM Paranormal First Time Dark Romance

MF Titles are published under Raven Kitts

www.ingramcontent.com/pod-product-compliance
Ingram Content Group UK Ltd.
Pitfield, Milton Keynes, MK11 3LW, UK
UKHW040007200726
13854UKWH00001B/79

9 798223 985655